On the map, the airport was a sprawling complex with numerous concourses branching out from the main terminal like long, curving spider legs. Soojin's eyes were fixed on the one little circle that said, *You are here.*

She didn't want to be here.

In an airport.

In Chicago.

They'd just gotten off a plane from New York to transfer to their fourteen-hour flight to Seoul, and her mother scoured the map as she muttered, "Gate B17." Soojin ignored her. She kept staring at the little circle.

"I am here, but not for long," Soojin whispered as she traced the circle with her finger.

Traci Chee
Mike Chen
Meredith Ireland
Mike Jung
Erin Entrada Kelly
Minh Lê
Grace Lin
Ellen Oh
Linda Sue Park
Randy Ribay
Christina Soontornvat
Susan Tan

YOU ARE HERE

HERE

CONNECTING FLIGHTS

Edited by Ellen Oh

Allida

An Imprint of HarperCollinsPublishers

Allida is an imprint of HarperCollins Publishers.

Library of Congress Cataloging-in-Publication Data
Names: Oh, Ellen, editor.
Title: You are here : connecting flights / edited by Ellen Oh.
Description: First edition. | New York : Clarion Books, [2023] | Audience:
    Ages 8–12. | Audience: Grades 4–6. | Summary: "Twelve young Asian
    Americans cross paths, meeting challenges and victories, in a busy air-
    port"—Provided by publisher.
Identifiers: LCCN 2022029573 | ISBN 9780063239098 (pbk.)
Subjects: LCSH: Short stories, American. | Asian Americans—Fiction. |
    CYAC: Short stories. | Airports—Fiction. | Asian Americans—Fiction. |
    LCGFT: Short stories.
Classification: LCC PZ5 .Y64 2023 | DDC [Fic]—dc23
LC record available at https://lccn.loc.gov/2022029573

Typography by Jessie Gang
23 24 25 26 27 LBC 5 4 3 2 1

First paperback edition, 2024

To anyone who has ever wondered if they belong,
we see you and know that you do.

1

Paul

With a line this long, you'd think we were waiting to get into Disney World, or Six Flags, or something cool. But no. We are at the airport, the place you go to wait in line for *more waiting*.

It's ten thirty in the morning, and we're at Chicago Gateway International Airport four hours early for our thirty-one-hour trip to Thailand. Once we get through this security line, we will wait at our gate, then wait in the boarding line, then wait on the plane, then do it all over again at another airport before we finally land in Bangkok.

At least Mom is feeling really proud of herself. She woke me up at the unholy hour of 5:30 a.m. so we could get a good parking spot. "See, Paul?" she said to me when our minivan pulled into the garage. "The Saturday before Fourth of July. Told you it would be crowded."

I have to admit that she's right. This security line snakes all the way back to the counter where we waited (yes, more waiting!) to check our suitcases and my little sister's car seat.

The other travelers are all on edge. Outside, what started as a summer drizzle is now a full-on thunderstorm. The sky is a spooky gray-green color, and thick sheets of rain lash the big glass windows of the terminal. Lightning flashes, and everyone sucks in their breath, then worriedly checks the flight information screens. When the sliding doors swoosh open, sopping-wet travelers hurry inside to the departure area, shivering from the shock of the air-conditioning. Our family is dry because we've been inside this airport since the beginning of time.

Beside me, Grandma is bundled up like we're going to scale Mount Everest. I tug on the sleeve of her lime-green puffy coat to get her attention. She's only one inch taller than me, and with her hood cinched tight around her brown face, I feel like I'm talking to a giant, plump caterpillar. "Grandma, the line is moving up," I say to her in Thai. "Here, let me help carry your bag."

"No, no, I got it." She hoists her faded cloth carry-on bag onto her shoulder. It's purple with red flowers, and it's almost as big as she is. "Your parents are the ones who need help."

Ahead of us, Mom and Dad are on full Jessie duty. My

three-year-old sister has round cheeks, big dark eyes, and pigtails that stick straight out like puppy dog ears. She's like what animators study when they're learning how to draw cute things. The adults around us smile and make peekaboo faces at her. She sticks out her tongue and scowls at them. She's a terror.

"Another cookie!" she whines as she clutches my dad's leg.

"Jessie, baby, don't you want to save those for the plane?" he says in the tone of voice you'd use to negotiate a hostage crisis.

"Nooooo!" she wails, throwing herself onto the floor.

I pull my black baseball cap down and act like I have no idea who this diabolical toddler is. At least during our flight Jessie will be sitting with Mom and Dad, and I'll get to chill with Grandma in our own row. Our total flying time will be twenty-two hours, and I plan to spend all of them watching movies and sipping ginger ale. Maybe if we're lucky, Jessie will get left on the plane, and we can carry on with our lives.

"Okay, Grandma, let's talk movies. You have to watch at least two with me before you fall asleep. I checked the airline website, and they don't have Star Trek reruns, but they do have the new Star Trek film, and—Grandma, are you even listening?"

"Huh? Oh, sure, Paul. You know I love Star Trek."

Grandma's usually so with it, but this morning she's distracted. It must be all the people. I look around at the other passengers crammed in with us. A group of about a dozen older boys has just joined the end of the line. Even with their clothes soaked with rainwater, they are the coolest guys I've ever seen. They look maybe high school age, and they're wearing matching red-and-white warm-ups. Their sneakers are so white they burn my eyeballs. Even before I notice the embroidered *Perez, DDS* basketball logo, I can tell they play basketball from the swagger-y way they swing their arms. When the line shifts and I can see them better, I realize they're all Asian American. Even cooler. I've never seen an all-Asian basketball team before.

Jessie lets out a screech, and I cringe. Luckily, the players are all too busy showing each other stuff on their phones to notice. With a squeal, Jessie runs away from the line. Mom sprints after her and just barely catches the ribbon on the waist of her yellow dress, pulling her back like a dog on a leash.

Darn. There goes my chance at being an only child again.

I hear a commotion directly behind us. I turn and see a woman in a bright pink sweater towing a shiny rolling bag. Her clothes and blond hair are probably usually perfect, but right now they hang limply, wet from the rain. Her son also looks soaked through. He dabs at his high-end sneakers with a wad of paper towels.

"Excuse me," the lady in pink says sweetly to the people in line. "We've got to get through security so we can buy some dry clothes before our flight. Do you mind if we get in front of you? Thanks!" She and her son slide ahead before the people even have a chance to answer.

As Pink Lady makes her way toward us, Grandma leans closer to me. "What's all that about?"

"They want to cut in line," I explain in Thai. Even though she loves watching American television, Grandma has never learned to speak English. "The lady in pink says she needs to go shopping for dry clothes before her plane leaves."

Grandma throws me a wink. "Let me handle this Klingon."

When Pink Lady comes up to us and does her whole skipping-the-line routine, Grandma plops her flower bag down right in the woman's way. She looks up and smiles at Pink Lady. "Sorry. No understand," she says in choppy English.

I have to bite my lip to keep from smiling as Grandma stands her ground like a bored water buffalo. Pink Lady has no choice but to stay where she is.

But unlike Grandma, I understand English perfectly. So I hear every word when Pink Lady whispers loudly to her son, "Just our luck that we'd get stuck behind *these people*. They slow everything down."

I bite my lip harder. My mind does that thing it always does when I hear something like this. It starts coming up with all the things she could have meant by "these people." Maybe she meant short people, people with demonic toddlers, people with grandmas who are dressed like arctic explorers.

But even as I'm making excuses for her, I know exactly what she meant. She meant Asian, Immigrant, Other. And then, even though I love my family and I'm proud of being Thai, and even though I know that *she* is the one with the problem, I feel the embarrassment start to creep up the back of my neck and fold itself around my face. It didn't even take this woman a full minute to stick our family into our own separate category: *these people*.

The line shifts, and I shuffle forward, then backtrack to get Grandma. She's looking into her bag and whispering to herself.

That flush of embarrassment surges higher. "Hey, Grandma, we've got to move up," I whisper. "Here, let me carry that for you." I take her bag and look down inside it. "This is heavy. What have you got in here?" Nestled between her extra sweaters, snacks, and Thai language magazines, there's a gigantic red plastic tub of instant coffee. "Coffee? You know we can get that in Thailand, right?"

I start to pull it out, but Grandma grabs my arm and shakes her head. She looks over her shoulder, like she doesn't want Mom and Dad to hear.

"Grandma, what is it?"

She leans in and whispers, "It's your grandfather."

For a moment, I get sad, thinking that Grandma must be reminiscing about Granddad, who passed away a little over a year ago. But then it hits me.

I look into the bag. I look at Grandma.

Oh no.

"Grandma," I whisper. "Did you bring Granddad's *ashes* to the airport?"

She reaches into the bag and pulls out the coffee container, cradling it in her arms. "I want to keep him safe."

"So you put him in a *coffee can*?"

She shrugs. "What? He likes coffee."

She carefully pops off the plastic lid and holds the can out for me to see. My heart is pounding, and I wince, expecting to see—I don't know, a bunch of gray powder and maybe a finger bone? Instead, inside the can is a polished wooden box with a lid of stained glass.

I shield Grandma with my body as I glance over my

shoulder at Pink Lady. Who knows what awful things she'd say if she knew what we were actually carrying?

Grandma hands the coffee canister back to me. "I had that box made just for him. It's prettier than the one we got from the temple. He should have something beautiful while he waits."

"Waits for what?" I ask, pushing the container deep, so deep, into the bottom of the bag.

"I'm taking him back home. To spread his ashes where the Chao Phraya River meets the sea. And then his spirit can be free and at peace."

Grandma talks about Granddad in the present tense, like he still lives with us. I know she misses him every day, but I was never close to him like I am to her. He never talked much, not even in Thai, and he never did get into Star Trek. But before he got sick, when he could still walk, he would take me to the park and teach me how to fly kites, Thai-style. He would soak our kite strings in glue and then roll them through the remains of a broken soda bottle, coating the strings in tiny shards of glass. Then we would battle, each of us trying to slice through the other's kite strings with our own. Way cooler than throwing a ball around.

I snap back to the present.

Focus, Paul. You've got your grandfather in a bag slung

over your shoulder. What's your strategy here?

Every time we go to Thailand, the airport officials ask us if we "have anything to declare," which means that we get one last chance to tell them what we're carrying. You can get in big trouble if you try to sneak things into another country that you're not supposed to bring. I try to remember the sign we passed when we entered the line. It said absolutely no firearms, lighters, or blades, but did it say anything about ashes? Do they let human remains just roll on through the scanner with everybody's toothbrushes and laptops?

"Grandma, shouldn't we tell the security people about this?"

She shakes her head vigorously. "These American guards won't know how to treat your grandfather. They probably would put him under the shoes, or something dirty like that! No, no. This is best. The bag will go through, and then we get him on the other side. Everything is a piece of cake after that."

I swallow and look up at my parents. Grandma and Granddad moved from Thailand to live with us after I was born, but Mom has lived in the US since she was a high school foreign exchange student. She and Grandma are always butting heads about doing things "old style" or "new style." I'm pretty sure I already know the answer when

I ask, "Mom and Dad don't know about this, do they?"

"Humph, your mom doesn't understand," says Grandma with a click of her tongue. "She wants her daddy to stay close to her, in Chicago. But it's too cold here in the winter! Your grandfather hates the cold. He needs to be in the place where his heart belongs, and that's in Thailand." Grandma puts her hand under my chin. "This will be a good trip for you, Paul. You can pay attention to all the little details so you know what to do when it's my time to go."

And then it hits me. Grandma is going to die someday. Then who will sit with me on the airplane? Who will peel baby oranges for me and Jessie, and hand us each segment like a precious jewel? Who will tell me stories about growing up along the river in Prachin Buri, fishing for eels in the reeds, riding in a rowboat to get to school?

The back of my throat squeezes up. I feel so stupid that not until this very moment, waiting in line at the airport, have I even considered that Mom and Dad will be gone someday, too. So will I. And where will our ashes be scattered? I've only been to Thailand twice. One day in the future, will someone smuggle me through security in a peanut butter jar?

Before I can get upset, I feel Grandma move toward me. She has always had this sixth sense for knowing what I'm thinking. She cups my face with her warm, dry hands.

"Hey, hey, don't be sad. You have a very long time before you need to worry about any of this stuff. And you know where *your* heart belongs, right?"

"Where?"

Grandma smiles so big that her whole face wrinkles up. "Right here! In Chicago, USA. You're my darling American grandson, and that makes me so proud." She hugs me close to her. "And no matter where we end up, our spirits will find each other. And watch Star Trek reruns together."

I hug her back, and even through her puffy caterpillar coat I can feel how strong she is despite being so small. I take a deep breath and inhale her scent: eucalyptus oil and talcum powder.

We're interrupted by Pink Lady, who taps me on the shoulder and says loudly in a fake Asian accent, "LINE MOVING. GO UP NOW."

There's another Asian American kid standing in line with his dad a couple rows over. Did he hear the racism in Pink Lady's comment? The line shifts, and the boy moves out of my sight.

And then I realize that we are finally almost at the front of the line. My stomach starts to flip. If we're going to come clean about these ashes, this is the time to do it.

I can hear Pink Lady's sandaled foot tapping impatiently behind me. I can just imagine the fit she'd throw if we slowed down the line by explaining what's going on. I know I shouldn't care about someone like her, but if we slow things down, then we'll prove that all her stereotypes about "these people" are right. I don't want her to be right. I just want to get through this without anyone noticing us.

I hold my breath as Dad hands the TSA agent our passports. This agent looks younger than all the others. His cheeks have a red rash, like he pushed down too hard with his razor when he was shaving. He doesn't smile as he looks at our documents and compares them to our plane tickets. He doesn't even smile at Jessie, and everyone smiles at Jessie.

Dad waits patiently, but I see the muscle in his cheek bouncing, and I know that he's feeling frustrated that things are taking so long. Now I'm extra glad I kept quiet about the ashes. Maybe Grandma's right, and we'll coast by with no one noticing us.

After what seems like forever, the rashy agent waves us through, and I let out a big breath.

Grandma and I go ahead of my parents to the X-ray machine. I let Grandma hold my arm while she slips off her shoes. I take mine off. I lay my backpack onto the conveyor belt and then her flower bag. I make sure her bag is nowhere near our shoes. In Thai culture, feet and shoes are dirty. They shouldn't touch something sacred or important.

Behind us, Mom and Dad start taking off their shoes, emptying their pockets, and hauling their carry-on bags up onto the conveyor belt. Jessie howls when Mom takes her precious light-up sneakers just as a TSA agent informs Dad that kids her age don't have to remove their shoes. I wince and look away.

Grandma squeezes my arm and smiles at me before walking through the body scanner.

Okay, here we go. I walk through the scanner. No alarms. No flashing lights. A huge wave of relief washes over me. Just a few more steps and we are home free.

I hand Grandma her shoes when they roll down the conveyor belt. I get mine. I grab my backpack.

I'm reaching for Grandma's bag when the conveyor belt pauses.

And then rolls backward.

The security agent running the machine leans in close to her screen, squinting. She runs the belt forward again, then backward again.

My heart turns into an ice cube.

The woman waves to another TSA agent to come over.

The agent, a tall man with graying hair and a badge that reads HASLEY, picks up the bag and starts saying something to Grandma. But I don't hear it, because there is a loud whooshing noise in my head, which must be the sound you hear just before you start having a panic attack.

As Dad walks through the body scanner, he says, "Paul, go help your grandma, okay?"

I follow Grandma and Agent Hasley to a side area with a metal table. Back at the conveyor belt, Jessie is now screaming about having to put her shoes *on*. People are looking at my parents and shaking their heads. I wish I could disappear or turn into vapor and just float away.

But I can tell from the look on Grandma's face that she doesn't understand what the agent is saying. I can't leave her.

". . . going to search your bag now," Agent Hasley says mechanically. "Please do not touch your bag or your belongings during this process."

The agent reaches into the bag. He pulls out the coffee canister. His eyebrows go up when he gets the lid off. He takes out the dark wooden box.

Suddenly, I feel a surge of energy beside me. Grandma's body is a blur as she lunges forward and claws at the agent's hands.

"Don't touch him! Don't open it!" she shouts in Thai, trying to snatch the box from him.

That's when my mind kicks into some strange superhero mode, and I can see everything happening in slow motion: the agent's confusion at why this tiny old woman has suddenly attacked him; my grandmother's single-minded goal—to protect her husband from being seized by these coldhearted strangers; her body as it twists, winding up her seventy-five-year-old muscles like a spring-loaded coil; and the agent's amusement, which is soon going to turn to anguish because he doesn't know what I know: *Grandma knows Muay Thai kickboxing, and when she was younger, she used to eat guys like him for breakfast.*

"WAIT!" I cry, leaping in between the two of them with my hands out.

Agent Hasley freezes. Grandma freezes. All hope of passing this checkpoint without being noticed has vanished. Everyone turns and stares. Behind us, the rashy-faced agent is shouting orders, stopping all passengers from entering the screening area. The entire checkpoint is in chaos.

Pink Lady screeches in fury as another agent stops her from walking through the body scanner and makes her join the other security line. She is pointing at us, yelling, her face turning the same color as her sweater.

I can't hear what she's saying, and I don't care. I turn my back on her and focus on what's really important.

I look up at Agent Hasley and firmly say, "Sir, my grand-mother doesn't speak English. Please let me explain . . ."

I force myself to speak slowly as I tell him everything about the ashes and about Thai culture so that I don't leave anything out. I try to look calm for Grandma's sake, but when I get to the part about worrying that they will confiscate Granddad, I can hear my voice trembling. When I'm finished, the agent lets out a sigh.

"You're allowed to bring the ashes through security," he says. "We just ask that you tell us so we can handle them properly. You're not in trouble, and we're certainly not going to confiscate them."

"Really?" I squeak.

"Really." He leans forward and lowers his voice. "Honestly? This kind of stuff happens all the time."

"It does?"

Agent Hasley smiles. "Kid, I've got enough stories to write a book." He nods down at the wooden box. "This cover is made of leaded glass, so we weren't able to properly scan it. I'll have to do an additional screening by hand. But don't worry. Tell your grandmother I'll be very gentle."

I explain everything to Grandma in Thai. Again, it takes time to find the right words. She still looks skeptical. "It's okay," I say to her. "He'll be careful."

Finally, Grandma gives Agent Hasley a nod of agreement. He gently swipes the outside of the box with a plastic wand covered with a cloth tip. When he's done, he presents the box to Grandma with both hands and dips his head, sort of like a little bow. She nods back.

The agent pats my shoulder as he hands me the bag. "You're a good kid to protect your grandmother."

I smile. It's probably best that he doesn't know that I was actually protecting *him* from Grandma's flying fists of fury.

As the chaos at the checkpoint slowly clears up and the passengers resume filing through, we rejoin Mom and Dad, whose faces are full of worry.

Before Mom can say anything, I reach out and wrap my arms around her. And then, just like I did for Agent Hasley, I explain everything. "Don't be mad at Grandma, Mom. She just wanted to do the right thing for Granddad. And it *is* the right thing. You have to be where your heart belongs, you know?"

Mom hugs me tight, then holds her arms out to Grandma. They embrace, and Mom tenderly smooths her hands over the wooden box. Soon they are talking a mile a minute in Thai, crying, apologizing, and offering forgiveness to each other all at once. Dad squeezes both of my shoulders. Translation from his unspoken words: *I'm proud of you, son.*

We are all still circled up in a big group hug when I see Pink Lady and her kid stomp off toward their gate. "We'll never make our flight now!" she cries.

I wish I could say that I was the kind of person who

took no satisfaction in this. Guess I'm just not one of *those people.*

Grandma dries her eyes and carefully slides the wooden box back into the coffee container. I place it in the bottom of the bag. I pat the bag and whisper, "Don't worry, Grand-dad. We're taking you home."

Now it's time to find our gate. Only three hours and thirty-four minutes left to wait.

Grandma hooks her arm into mine. "I told you. Piece of cake."

"Hold on," says Mom, looking around frantically. *"Where's Jessie?"*

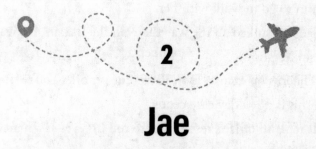

2

Jae

"What's this?"

Mr. Peters took one look at Jae, then glared at Mom. He was an average-sized white man with short brown hair and almost no chin. Jae saw that one of his eyes twitched a little, which made his glare almost comical.

It was time for the shift change; people were leaving the employee break room, either to start their work duties or to head home.

"I'm sorry, Richard," Mom said. "The sitter—"

Jae's usual babysitter was Gracie, a college student. Earlier that day, Gracie's grandmother had fallen and broken her hip, and Gracie had had to take her to the hospital. Mom had refused point-blank to discuss Jae's contention that he was old enough to stay home on his own. She couldn't afford to call in sick, so the only choice left was for him to go to work with her.

Jae had sulked all the way there on the L train. He was still sulking now.

"There's no excuse," Mr. Peters cut her off. "You're late. And this is not a day care center."

It took all of Jae's resolve not to roll his eyes as a match for the instant snark response inside his head. *Um, riiiiight. It's an airport.*

Mom lowered her head slightly, but her voice was steady. "You won't even know he's here," she said. "He's a good boy."

If I'm a good boy, how come I'm not allowed to stay at home on my own? Jae kept his face blank, but inside his head, he was scowling—because he knew the answer.

"Uses questionable judgment." "Lacks impulse control." That was grown-up-speak for the fact that Jae sometimes "made bad choices," which was why Mom was reluctant to leave him on his own.

It wasn't like he *wanted* to misbehave or rebel. But being good was slippery. It didn't stay still; it moved around, and not only that, sometimes it meant exactly opposite things. Like, there were times when being good meant speaking up, but other times when it meant staying quiet. The only thing Jae was sure of was that "good" was determined by whoever was in charge at the time. For today, Jae knew that good behavior would mean a serious stretch of boredom. Being bored was the worst.

Mr. Peters was talking. "I don't know how they do things where you come from, but this is a *professional establishment.* We do not bring children to work with us."

Scowl redirected at Mr. Peters. *Where we come from? That would be the West Side, off Cicero. And don't you talk to my mom like that. She's worked here way longer than you— she's the one who showed you around when you first started. And besides, she's older than you—can't you show a little respect?*

Of course, he said none of that aloud. This was a "staying quiet" moment.

Mr. Peters moved his glare from Mom to Jae himself, then seemed to hesitate. He reached out with his hand and rubbed Jae's head awkwardly.

"I'm sure this guy won't be a problem," he said, in a friendly voice so fake it made Jae cringe. "You'll just stay here and—and hold down the fort. Right, Jake?"

"It's *Jae.*" Jae and Mom spoke in unison.

The false smile dropped from Mr. Peters's face. He shrugged, clearly not interested in getting Jae's name right. "I should have you take him home and dock your pay," he said. "I'm making an exception just this once. See that it n't happen again." He banged the door as he left.

"Jerk," said Angie, one of Mom's work partners. She stood in the doorway of the cloakroom at the back and rolled her eyes. She must have overheard the whole conversation.

Now she gathered her purple-streaked hair into a ponytail. "C'mon, Myung, let's get started." She put a hand on Mom's shoulder. The two women moved toward the door together, Mom a head shorter than Angie.

Then Mom turned and hurried back toward Jae.

"I know you don't want to be here," she said quietly. "I'm sorry I couldn't work out anything else. But please just stay here and wait for me. I might be able to come back for a few minutes on my break." She looked at him pleadingly, then gave his arm a quick squeeze before leaving with Angie.

Jae glanced around the room. It was a fairly large space, with worn vinyl couches around the periphery, square tables and plastic chairs, a counter along one wall with a sink flanked by two refrigerators, a row of vending machines. To the right of the counter was the door to the cloakroom, where there were two restrooms and a couple rows of lockers.

In the main room, there were four television screens. Two were tuned to a news channel; the other two showed closed-circuit footage from cameras throughout the airport.

Jae knew the airport inside and out. Mom had worked here since he was a toddler, and for years he had come along with Dad to pick her up at the end of her shifts. They came early whenever they could so Jae could play. If the airport wasn't busy, he was allowed to run in the big open spaces. As a little kid, he had especially loved the escalators, going up and down over and over. He had a clear memory of Mom showing him how to step on and off all by himself.

Jae crossed the room to sit on the couch that was closest to the closed-circuit TV monitors. The images on the screens changed every fifteen seconds, cycling through different parts of the airport. On the rare occasions Jae was in the break room, he always tested himself: How quickly could he identify the exact location of the shots on the screens?

Front lobby, Delta desk.

Terminal 1, Concourse B food court, Dragon Lotus counter.

Baggage claim, United carousel, Terminal 2.

After a while, he got out his tablet and played the latest *Zelda* game. Then he watched a whole bunch of animal videos—some funny, some amazing. He got up to stretch his legs and use the restroom.

Still not even halfway through Mom's shift. Was there

anything more boring than waiting?

As he swiped idly at his tablet, he happened to glance at the monitors. The left-hand screen—*TSA checkpoint, Terminal 1*—something was going on there.

Jae sat up and looked more closely. A few uniformed officers were gathering around the screening area. Their attention seemed to be directed toward the end of the conveyor belt, where several people were clustered. Jae could see a couple, an older woman, and two kids. One was a boy about his own age, the other a little girl maybe three or four years old. They all had dark hair. *Asian*, Jae decided.

The image disappeared. He didn't have to wait long for it to show up again. Within seconds, it became clear that something was wrong. The screens showed crowds of people moving around. Jae pieced together what was happening: one of the two lines at the TSA checkpoint had been closed down, and everyone from that line was being shunted into the other queue.

What was going on?

Jae kept watching. Again he saw the Asian family—but this time, the little girl wasn't with the others. She had wandered a few steps away, toward the benches where people could sit while they put their shoes back on. The girl hippity-hopped past the benches. Jae could see tiny flashes of light at her feet; he realized that she was wearing those light-up sneakers.

The images changed. A few moments later, Jae saw the girl's back as she toddled away. He frowned in concentration at the monitor. The girl's family, distracted by whatever was happening with the TSA agents, hadn't noticed her disappearance. She was out of sight now, headed into the big central hall from which the gate concourses branched off.

Jae's heart boomed in his chest. A powerful memory assailed him: getting separated from his mom in a big-box store when he was about five years old. He had been wandering the aisles, singing tunelessly, when he looked up and realized that his mother was no longer in sight. He would never forget the panic that had surged through him: it had felt like the end of the world.

For a long time after that, Jae insisted on riding in the shopping cart so he wouldn't get separated from his parents again. He had been too big for the seat; he'd had to ride in the cart itself. Years later, talking to his mom about the incident, he had been astounded to learn that he had been lost for no more than a couple of minutes.

Anytime now, that little girl would look around and see that her family had vanished. She would feel that same terrible stomach-turning, heart-squeezing panic. . . . And he was the only one who knew where she was.

Jae didn't pause to think any further. He leapt from his seat and ran to the door.

♀ ♀ ♀

The break room was about a third of the way down Concourse B, tucked away behind a nondescript door that said Employees Only. Jae yanked open the door. Through the big windows on the opposite wall, he saw that it was raining. Pouring, actually. He hadn't noticed before, because the break room had no windows. As if to add to the drama, there was a blaze of lightning, followed almost immediately by an enormous thunderclap.

Jae tore through the concourse, staying next to the wall, where there were fewer pedestrians. The closer he got to the central hall, the more crowded it became. Jae dodged and deked his way through the clusters and knots of people. For the briefest of moments, one part of his mind realized that he was enjoying himself—it was fun trying to get past everyone without tripping or bumping into them. Almost like a video game come to life.

When he reached the entrance to the hall, Jae stopped so suddenly that he almost tripped. Stunned, he stared at the sea of people in front of him.

He had never seen it this crowded! People were packed together so tightly he could barely see the floor. He glanced up at the flight information screens that hung from the ceiling.

DELAYED
CANCELED
DELAYED
CANCELED
CANCELED
CANCELED

Jae saw through the big ceiling skylights that the storm had worsened; obviously flights were being affected by the weather. People were upset, bewildered, angry. Every single person over the age of about twelve was talking on a cell phone. The vast space in the hall was filled with the sound of voices. Miserable voices.

"My flight was just canceled!"

"Is it the weather?"

"—storms are terrible, AND the security line just closed down—"

"—no other flights today?!"

Jae took a deep breath. To get across the big hall toward

where he had seen the girl on the monitor, he would have to go through that crowd. For the first time since he had jumped up from the couch, Jae realized what he had done: he'd left the break room against explicit orders from both Mom and Mr. Peters. If he ran into either of them, there would be no way to hide his disobedience. Worse yet, he might get Mom in trouble.

Should he turn around and go back? But what about the little girl?

Jae squared his shoulders and began making his way through the crowd.

♀ ♀ ♀

There was no running now; he jostled past people a step at a time. He also had to keep shifting his sight line—down low, to try to spot the girl or her flashing sneakers; higher, to make sure he didn't run into people.

"Excuse me. Excuse me. Sorry," he repeated over and over. "Sorry—I need to get by—excuse me—"

"HEY! HEY, YOU!"

A shrill voice rose above the cacophony. Jae recoiled before he even knew who had spoken; he knew instinctively that the voice was yelling at *him*.

A woman emerged from behind the nearest clump of people. It was someone he didn't know, a short and stocky woman with reddish hair and very pale skin.

Then Jae saw that she was holding a child by the hand, half dragging her.

Light-up sneakers, check. Also, chubby cheeks and high pigtails. It was definitely the little girl he was looking for.

"Is this your sister?" the woman snapped. "Are you supposed to be taking care of her? She was all by herself—you need to keep an eye on her!"

Sister? Jae frowned, but in the next breath, realization hit him. *She thinks it's my sister . . . because we're both Asian.*

"She's not—" Jae started to speak, but the woman steamrolled right over him.

"You're big enough to know better," she scolded. "She could have gotten lost—what were you thinking?"

The little girl had been quiet, but the woman's anger was apparently upsetting her, and she started to cry.

"You take her right back to your parents," the woman ordered.

In the time it took the woman to finish that sentence, the girl's cries went from zero to sixty. She was screaming now, pulling her hand away from the woman's grip.

It was one of those confusing moments. Ignoring a grown-up was disrespectful, and that wasn't good, but Jae had tried to tell her the truth, and she hadn't listened. Did that make it okay to ignore her now?

Probably not. He had left the break room despite

Mom's plea and was now about to ignore an adult. *At least I'm being consistent with the bad choices*, he thought. Funny not funny.

He turned away from the woman, went down on one knee, and held his hand out toward the girl.

"Hi there," he said softly. "I'm Jae. What's your name?"

Jae was an only child, but he had two little cousins whom he often looked after during family gatherings. He had used this tactic with them, just as Mom had with him when he was little. Whenever he had cried hard, she had lowered her voice to a whisper. He had had to stop crying, or at least lower the volume, to hear what she was saying.

The girl eyed him suspiciously for a moment, but sure enough, she stopped crying. "J-Jessie," she said, her voice catching on sobs.

Jae kept his voice down. "Hey, Jessie. How about we go find your mama?"

"Mama? Paul?" She toddled closer to Jae and let him pick her up.

Jae was about to correct her—*I'm Jae, not Paul*—when he realized that she was asking about the other kid, most likely her brother.

A man pushed his way through the crowd to stand next to the woman. "Sandy, what's going on?" he asked. "We have to get these flights straightened out!"

"Stewart! What the—why did you get out of line?"

"I didn't know where you went—"

"It wasn't my fault. This little girl, her brother wasn't looking after her. She was all on her own, and she ran right into me." She turned back to Jae. "As if things aren't bad enough with this chaos—now we've lost our place in line!"

And that's supposed to be my problem? Jae bit back the words and swallowed hard before he spoke. "She's not my sister."

The woman looked confused for a moment, then scowled. "What do you mean, she's not your sister?"

Meanwhile, Jessie had calmed down and was singsonging a little chant almost right into his ear. "Paul ball all. Tall doll Paul." It might have been cute any other time, but right now Jae could hardly hear himself think.

"It's okay," he said, his body tensing as he tried to focus. "I know where her parents are. I'll just take her—"

"Wait a minute," said Stewart. "If she's not your sister, you're not going anywhere with her. I've read about this—"

He looked around at the folks within earshot. "Those illegals. They bring kids who aren't related and make them pretend to be siblings—it's one of their schemes to get in without being documented."

Jae was now utterly confused. What on earth was the man talking about?

"You stay right there," Stewart said sternly. "Sandy, I'll keep an eye on them—you go get someone from security."

Sandy flapped her hand at him. "Security? Look at this mess!" she said, her voice almost a shout. "I can barely move, it's so crowded. Security! No way—"

"Well, they're the ones who have to look into this," Stewart was saying.

As he spoke, Jae noticed that people nearby were responding to what they had heard—or misheard.

"Someone wants security—"

"—illegals, that's what I heard—"

"Security? Was there an announcement?"

"Is there some kind of threat? As if this weather weren't bad enough!"

Jae could hardly believe his ears. Security? A threat? How had this happened? All he had wanted to do was to help get the girl back to her family!

He was still holding Jessie, who was clearly getting restless. She kept plucking at the collar of his T-shirt, saying "Paul, ball, doll" with each pluck.

He glanced around and saw that he was surrounded. Even more people were packed into the space now. There was no way he could make a break for it.

Then Sandy spoke again, her voice shriller than before. "Stewart, this is *not* our problem. We have to figure out how we're getting to Tampa! Come on."

"Sandy—"

"Stewart, are you coming?"

The woman cast one more disdainful look at Jae, then began making her way toward the long lines for customer service. Her husband followed her, and Jae let out a sigh of relief.

"Okay, Jessie," he said. "Let's go find your family."

♀ ♀ ♀

Jae's relief lasted no longer than a few moments. As he turned to make his way toward the screening checkpoint where he had last seen Jessie's family, he saw that Stewart and Sandy had somehow encountered two airport security guards. Sandy was talking, and Stewart was pointing— straight at Jae.

Jae took a quick look around. Too crowded to run. No way to melt into the crowd, either—not enough Asian people there. All he could do was hope that the guards would listen and believe him.

One guard was a woman with copper curls escaping from under her cap; her name badge said MARTINEZ. The other was a Black man with a mustache, ROBINSON. Both looked at him sternly.

"Is that your sister?" Robinson asked.

Jae shook his head. "No, sir."

It seemed like the right moment to show respect by saying "sir." He could feel his heart throbbing—he hadn't known how hard it was to talk to someone in uniform, even if you hadn't done anything wrong. Well, at least not anything *illegal.*

"Then what are you doing with her?"

"I—I—she's lost," he said, his face burning. "I'm trying to help her find her family."

"What's your name?" asked Martinez.

"Jae. Jae Han. My mom works here."

Robinson's expression changed at once. "You're Myung's kid?"

Jae nodded, feeling his heartbeat slow down a little.

"Myung?" Martinez said. "She the one who makes those—those rice-roll things?"

"Kimbap." Robinson nodded. "Man, I wish I had some right now."

Despite the chaos all around and inside his own head, Jae had to smile. He had been rolling kimbap with Mom since he was barely bigger than Jessie. Mom was famous for her kimbap. Sometimes she made dozens of rolls and brought them to work to share with her colleagues.

Jae saw his opening. "Officers? This is Jessie. Her family was at the security checkpoint. Can I—is it okay if I take her there now?"

He hoisted Jessie higher up on his hip; his arms were getting tired. She had stopped tugging on his T-shirt, but now she was shaking her head back and forth, the ends of her pigtails hitting his face. *Thwack-thwack-thwack.* It was half hilarious and all annoying.

"Paul ball doll," she chanted, one word for each *thwack.* "Paul ball doll, all Paul tall."

The officers looked at each other. "No, we'll do it," Martinez said. But when she stepped forward, Jessie shook her head harder and tightened her arms around Jae's neck so much he could barely breathe.

Robinson shrugged. "Go ahead and walk them over there," he said to Martinez. "I'll get in touch with Myung."

Great. Just great.

Jae had been hoping to return the girl to her family and then get back to the break room before anyone noticed he was gone. Now Mom would find out for sure that he had disobeyed her.

He didn't want to think about it. *Get Jessie back to her family and then figure things out.*

Martinez led Jae and Jessie toward the security checkpoint. When they were almost there, Jae set Jessie down on the floor.

"Phew," he said, "you're heavy. I think you might weigh more than me."

Jessie giggled. Craning his neck, Jae could see her family, including a boy a few years older than he was—the same one he'd seen on the monitor earlier.

"That must be Paul," he said to Jessie.

"Paul!" Jessie shrieked. "Paul Paul *Paaaaaaaul!*" She ran toward the boy, jumped into his arms, and grabbed both of his ears, tugging on them. Apparently, that was her idea of a hug.

Commotion and babble followed. Paul put Jessie down, and everyone crowded around her. After a few moments, the mother turned to Martinez. "Are you the one who found her?" she asked.

"No, ma'am," Martinez replied. "It was this young man here." She jerked her chin toward Jae.

More babble as each person thanked Jae profusely. He couldn't decide if he was more pleased or embarrassed by all the attention. Only a few minutes earlier, that guy Stewart had practically accused him of being part of some kind of threat. Now Jessie's family was acting like he was a hero.

A hero about to get into big trouble with Mom . . .

Jae had turned to leave when Paul spoke to him.

"Thanks, man," Paul said. "I know she can be a—a handful."

"She was fine," Jae said, "except she kept doing this

rhyming thing. Like, 'Paul all doll.'"

Paul sighed. "She does that. It's so annoying."

"Um, maybe you could change your name," Jae said, "to something that's harder to rhyme. How about . . . Augustus?"

"Knowing Jessie, she'd figure out a way to rhyme it somehow," Paul said with a shrug.

"Baugustus," Jae suggested.

"Zaugustus."

"Shmaugustus."

They grinned at each other, then said goodbye as Paul walked back to his family. Jae watched them for a few seconds longer and was relieved to see that Jessie was now stamping her feet to make her shoes light up; she seemed to have completely forgotten what had happened.

That's okay, Jae thought. *I'll remember for both of us.*

Mom was waiting outside the door to the break room. "Thanks," she said to the officers. "I owe you."

"We'll take payment in kimbap," Robinson joked.

"You got it."

The officers left. Mom marched Jae through the door.

"Okay," she said. "This better be good."

On the walk back to the break room, Jae had conjured

and discarded a dozen explanations to try to get out of trouble, even as he knew that none of them would work. Mom always saw through lies.

So I might as well tell the truth?

Of course, telling the truth hadn't gone well with Sandy and Stewart. Jae was still shaken by how quickly they had assumed things about him, and how fast those things had blown up into what could have been *real* trouble. When all along he'd just been trying to help Jessie. If he told the truth now, would Mom understand?

"Okay," he said, looking at the floor. He took a breath. "What happened was . . ."

He started at the beginning—with seeing Jessie and her family on the monitors—and told her everything. He spoke quickly, glancing up at her from time to time. When he got to the part about Sandy and Stewart, he thought he saw her frown briefly, but she said nothing, so he kept going.

"I know I was supposed to stay here," Jae said, "but I— I didn't stop to think, Mom. I saw her on the monitor, and I remembered that time I got lost when I was little—I had to do something."

She was quiet for a moment. "Well—"

Just then Mr. Peters burst into the room. "What's going on? Why aren't you on Concourse E? Is it because of what

I've been hearing?" He pointed accusingly at Jae.

Uh-oh. What exactly had Mr. Peters heard? If it was anything like Stewart's version, Jae could be in big trouble. And what if Mom got in trouble, too? That would be beyond unfair—it wasn't her fault at all.

"Security said there was trouble at checkpoint A," Mr. Peters was saying, his voice rising in anger. "Something about Asians! Did you have anything to do with that? You were told to stay right here—"

"Richard, please."

Jae looked up in surprise at the sound of Mom's voice. It was ice cold and steel hard.

"It's true that Jae has been disobedient. But he is my child, not yours. It is up to me to discipline him."

Mr. Peters's pink face turned magenta, and his eyes bugged out. Clearly, he was shocked by Mom's tone of voice. Jae held his breath. If Mom lost her job, it would be because of him. . . .

Mom spoke again over the sound of Mr. Peters's sputtering.

"Richard, with all the cancellations and delays, the facilities and the public areas are going to be very heavily used, probably right through tomorrow. The duty roster and the supply inventory need to be adjusted, don't they?"

Mr. Peters blinked. For a moment, he looked a little

lost. "Yes. Yes, of course. I was just—I was going to get started on that—"

Then he seemed to collect himself and glared at Jae. "I don't expect to have to check on you again, young man. Is that clear?"

Jae nodded.

"We're done here, Myung. Get over to E." Mr. Peters was back to his old pompous self. "And check the portal—I'll have the adjusted roster and inventory up shortly."

Jae watched him leave. To his surprise, he heard Mom let out a sigh of obvious relief.

Had Mom been worried about standing up to Mr. Peters? She certainly hadn't seemed scared—her voice hadn't wobbled a single bit.

"You better call your dad," she said. "Tell him to come get you when he's finished at work. I'll be doing a double shift tonight."

Jae pictured Mom heading to Concourse E, which would be full of anxious, unhappy travelers. She would do her best to keep the restrooms and common areas tidy, to make things a little more convenient and comfortable for them. The inconsiderate ones would leave a mess, which she would clean up again. And again.

He thought of one thing that might help. "Should I ask

Dad to bring you something to eat?" Mom got the employees' discount at the food court, but he knew she liked her own homemade dishes more—a lot more.

"Good idea," she said. "There's some leftover kimchi jjigae in the fridge." She gave him a quick hug, then headed for the door.

Jae realized that she hadn't said anything about disciplining him, and he wasn't about to remind her.

Mom had one hand on the door lever when she turned back toward him. "Jae? You didn't stay here like you were supposed to, but I know you were trying to do the right thing. I'm proud of you."

The door closed behind her.

Jae walked to one of the tables and sat down. Whew, he was tired. He pulled another chair a little closer and put his feet up on the seat. Seeing his sneakers, he smiled—from now on, he knew he would think of Jessie whenever he saw light-up sneakers.

Mom was proud of him.

Even though Mr. Peters had been furious.

Jae shook his head. Good kid / troublemaker / threat / hero—all within less than half an hour. Who knew that coming to work with Mom would turn out like this? But maybe that was the way it was with a lot of things in life:

once you decided to do something, there was really no way to know for sure what would happen, or how people would react.

Which meant . . . what?

If you couldn't know for sure, all you could do was make your best guess. And then do your best. And hope for the best.

And that seemed like something he could work with.

3

Mindy

The Duolingo owl is a tyrant. Yes, language app, I know it's time for another Korean lesson, but after months and months, I'm still no good at it. And I doubt that'll change before takeoff.

Dads and I are at our second airport of the day. We flew out of New York this morning, and now we're stuck in Chicago. It's raining cats and dogs, so maybe we won't be able to fly to Seoul after all. I keep glancing at the departures board hoping to see the word "canceled."

DELAYED

Darn it.

"Hey, Mindy," Daddy Pat says. "You hungry? You should eat something before we board."

I shake my head no. I should be hungry, but my stomach is in knots. I just . . . it's complicated.

"Come on, let's go find something," Daddy Brian says.

He probably didn't catch my headshake. Or maybe he did, and I've been overruled. Not sure.

I sigh and follow them, squeaking my sneakers along the shiny floor.

We pass happy, excited families, and I wish I felt that way. It's not that I'm upset about leaving the country— I was stoked to go to Europe for the first time two summers ago. We spent weeks roaming around Ireland, where Daddy Pat's family is originally from. His second cousins took us around the Ring of Kerry, which was so pretty, and made us soda bread, which was so good. No leprechauns, which, at ten years old, I kinda sorta hoped were real, so that was a bummer. But we had such a good time I barely wanted to come back.

Then Scotland last year was even better. Daddy Brian's family is from there, and Edinburgh was like the coolest place ever. We did the big Ferris wheel, shopped on the Royal Mile with Great-Grandma Edna—who still lives there—hiked up Arthur's Seat, and toured a real castle.

But this summer it's "my turn." I was adopted from Korea when I was six months old, and my dads decided it's time to go explore where I'm from. They're super excited about me reconnecting with my Korean roots, but I don't know how to tell them I don't want to go. I've been working on it since they announced the trip at Christmas, and now it's almost the Fourth of July, and I'm in an airport, so . . . hasn't gone well.

I mean, there's nothing wrong with Korea. Or, actually, there is: they don't recognize same-sex marriage. My dads aren't sure how tolerant it is there, so they decided to pretend to not be together once we land. And I hate that. They hate that. A lot.

So, I don't know why we're going somewhere my dads can't be themselves, except that they said I should "experience it."

We reach an airport directory, and Daddy Brian wraps an arm around my shoulders. "Look at all these choices, Min."

"I'm not really hungry," I mumble to my shirt.

Daddy Pat rattles off the offerings. "Chipotle? Sushi? Oh, they have a P.F. Chang's To Go!"

I frown. P.F. Chang's *was* one of my favorites, but Lewis and Ann in my class made sure to point out that it's *American*, not Chinese food. They have Taiwanese and Chinese parents, and both bring in moon cakes for the Mid-Autumn Festival. They stared at me like I had three heads when I said I liked P.F. Chang's last year. Ann stuck up her nose and said it's fake Asian and asked why I didn't know that. But as far as I knew, P.F. Chang's was Chinese . . . ish.

I mean, it's not the authentic beef noodle soup Lewis's mom brought in for Food Heritage Day. And it's not the red bean buns Ann's dad baked. But it's tasty and definitely better than the bulgogi my dads tried to make. That turned out like soy shoe leather, so they sent me in with Korean BBQ takeout instead. I shifted the meat from the containers to a plate and hid the bags under the table before I presented it for the festival. Still, even though the food was delicious, I got a disappointed sigh from someone's granddad when I couldn't speak to him in Korean or use chopsticks. I hear it in Koreatown, too—that sound at the back of the throat, combined with a little headshake. Like I'm *that* generation—the one that lost touch with their roots. No one realizes my family's roots are Scottish and Irish American. That I don't remember Korea at all.

And now I have a month of disappointed sighs and lousy chopstick usage ahead of me. *Come on, mouth, work. Tell them you don't want to go.*

"Oh, look, Min, they have a Jamba Juice!" Daddy Brian taps the board with a big grin. His smile is always contagious.

I forget my worries for a second and give him a small smile. "Okay."

"Let's go!" Daddy Pat says.

We make our way to Jamba, passing a bunch of travelers, including a father carrying a little boy on his shoulders. Daddy Pat used to carry me that way when I was little. I felt like I was on top of the world. Right now . . . not so much.

When we get to the stand, I order my usual, a Strawberries Gone Bananas smoothie and an oatmeal bowl, but this time I go for extra honey and extra brown sugar crumbles. Maybe the sugar will help.

Dentist Daddy Pat side-eyes me, though. "Extra brown sugar?"

Daddy Brian elbows him before I can respond. "It's a travel day. Live a little."

They smile at each other, and Daddy Pat leans into Daddy Brian. They won't do that once we land, and I don't know why they're not more bothered by it. I am. I'm bothered by all of it.

I try to work up the courage to say something. I straighten my spine and push my shoulders back, but really, what's the point? It's way too late. We're literally in an airport. Our suitcases are somewhere waiting to be loaded on a Korea-bound plane.

I slouch. I had really hoped I'd change my mind. That with Duolingo lessons or time, I'd want to "reconnect" with Korea. Or feel any connection to it at all. Instead, I feel like I did when I was standing behind takeout on Ms. Segman's Food Heritage Day—like I'm faking it.

I should tell them.

I'm midthought when guards rush past us. Blue-on-blue uniforms blur by as they head for the security checkpoint.

My dads and I turn. Something is going on at TSA. I stand on my tiptoes, but I'm barely five feet tall. I can't see anything from here. My dads are both six feet and move a few steps closer. And then a few more. Daddy Brian is a reporter for the *New York Times* and "inquisitive"—which is a nice-people word for nosy.

Someone shouts at the security screening, and even the Jamba employees look and whisper.

Eventually everything dies down, and people come through the checkpoint again. Daddy Brian, inquisitive as ever, waves over the first family.

"Hey, what happened back there?" he asks. "Was there some kind of threat?"

A blond woman in a pink sweater stops, looking totally frazzled. "Yes, it was foreigners—Asians. Trying to smuggle something through. Hopefully they go back to their own country and stay there."

I stand like a statue, totally frozen as each word hits me.

Asians. Own country. Stay there.

Or, well, I freeze until Daddy Brian physically pulls me into their conversation with his hand on my back pushing me forward.

"I don't know what you're trying to say in front of our daughter. But I hope I didn't hear you correctly."

Oh no. I want to melt into the earth as the woman gives us a confused look.

"What?" she barks.

People rarely understand we're a family, and this woman definitely won't. Heat floods into my cheeks, and I'd really, really like to be . . . anywhere else.

I look to Daddy Pat for help, but he takes out his phone to record her.

"Yeah, do you want to repeat that?" he asks.

I wince. This is how they are. Confront hate! Don't let people feel safe saying bigoted things! Silence is violence! Stand up for what's right even when it makes everyone uncomfortable at Thanksgiving! They nearly got into a fight one Pride with some people who'd come to spoil it. But this is different. This isn't about them. It's about . . . me.

"Ugh, we're just late," the woman says. "We don't have time for this."

She holds up her hand to block Daddy Pat's phone. Then she grabs her son's hand and drags him away, but not before he quickly pulls his eyes at me.

"Kung Flu," he whispers.

My face tingles as blood drains out of it. I yank away from Daddy Brian, but my dads barely notice. They didn't see or hear the boy. Instead, they're talking to each other about that woman, patting themselves on the back for calling her out.

I wish they hadn't.

If they had just let it go, and the woman had left, I wouldn't feel like this. My heart is racing, and I want to scream and throw things, but I know I'll probably just cry. Which is so much worse.

Sure, I've heard things said about Asian people in passing in the city, on TV, etc. I know the stereotypes, like how we're always thought of as foreign even when we've been here for generations, but all my life I've also heard: "Well, *you're* not *really* Asian." And normally I kinda believe that. Lewis and Ann are. I'm kinda not. That's how it goes.

So even though I knew people called COVID-19 the "China virus" and there was violence toward Asian Americans during the pandemic, I never felt like it was aimed at me. I'd never had anyone say something like that to my face.

Until now.

Because my dads had dragged me into their confrontation with no thought to how I feel or what I want.

When I look to the side, there's a girl around my age also waiting for her order. I think she's white, but she looks concerned as she stares at me. She must've noticed the kid the same way I did.

I turn away. She has a kind face, but there's no way she can understand how I feel.

"You okay, Min? People like that . . . they're just garbage," Daddy Brian says. He shakes his head with disgust.

"It's ignorance and hate, and it's dying out," Daddy Pat adds.

They always say that. They talk about how attitudes have changed toward the gay community since they were young. But is hate dying out? That woman was teaching her son to be just like her.

My eyes sting, and it's all too much.

"I . . . I'm going to go find a bathroom," I say.

"Oh, okay," Daddy Pat says. But he purses his lips, his blue eyes looking troubled.

"We'll grab a table once the orders are ready," Daddy Brian says. "Just leave your bag and meet us there."

Same skeptical look in his brown eyes.

I give them my backpack and take off in whatever direction is away from them, away from the kid and the racist mom and confrontations I didn't ask for. I walk for a while, and then it's hard to see, because tears blur my vision.

Why hadn't I been able to say something like my dads? Why didn't I even want to? A bunch of super-late responses flood my head—things I should've said and done. But the truth is I'm not an in-your-face person. I'm not like my dads.

I continue until I find myself in a crowd of Asian travelers going the opposite way from me. They must be from the flight that just arrived from Beijing.

I accidentally bump into a man pulling a roller bag.

He stops and says something in . . . Mandarin maybe? I'm not sure. I apologize in English, and when he says something else, I give him a wide-eyed stare and shake my head. I hope this is universal for *I don't understand you*. A woman leans down and says something as well. She looks friendly, but I still can't understand her. She might be speaking Korean. I really don't know.

Ann would've. She speaks both Mandarin and Cantonese and goes to Chinese classes after school. She would've known what they were saying. She would've been able to apologize for running into them. She would've been happy to go to Asia to visit extended family. I'm not like her.

I turn around but stop, the blond lady's "What?" ringing in my ears. I'm not white like my dads, either.

So, am I just . . . nothing?

My vision blurs again, and now I'm knocking into

people like a sad little pinball, tripping over rolling bags and bumping into more travelers. I don't know where I'm going, because I have nowhere to go.

I catch a sign that says Charging Station. It's a little space between two walls. I dive out of the busy corridor and duck into a seat. I wipe my face with my hands, glad to be free of the crowd, but I know I'm literally hiding.

Ugh. I am not the stand-up-to-things type. I can't even tell my own dads how I feel. I'm just . . . a coward.

My insides twist, and disappointment makes my lungs heavy.

I go to plug in my phone, but then I remember it's in my backpack—with my dads.

I groan and sit, staring at nothing. I don't want to move, but I can't hide out here forever. Dads will get worried, and I can't message them.

With the deepest sigh, I get up and peek out. The mess I caused has cleared.

I walk out as though I hadn't gone through the corridor like a human wrecking ball. This time, I move with the crowd as I head back to Jamba.

I'm barely ten feet from the charging station when I see an elderly Asian couple pointing in opposite directions from each other. I think they're Filipino. They look like my friend from camp, Pamela. But unlike Pamela, who never worried about anything, this couple looks concerned. They keep gesturing around and looking at their watches. When I start past them, they stop me and say something in what I think is Tagalog.

I shake my head. I can't understand or respond to them, because, once again, I'm useless. I don't even have my phone, so it's not like I can ask the aggressive owl or Google Translate. I'm about to turn away when the old lady reaches out and rests a hand on my arm. Her eyes plead with me.

"I'm sorry," I say. "I can't understand you." I point to myself and then gesture up in the air and, *ugh*, please say that's not me talking louder and slower like that'll break a language barrier.

My shoulders slump, and I hang my head. She gently lifts my chin and smiles.

Something in her expression tells me she knows I can't understand, but she thinks I can help anyhow. She points at their boarding passes, tapping the paper multiple times. I take a look. They're heading to Saigon. Gate E37. We're at E37, and no one else is here. There must've been a gate change with the weather.

And then I realize I *can* help. I, at least, understand English. I wave them along to the departures board. I scan down with my finger and find Saigon. It's now Gate E2, and it's boarding.

"Two," I say, holding up two fingers. "Your gate is now E2, and you need to get there quick."

The old man knits his eyebrows, and the woman shakes her head. They have no idea what I'm saying.

What am I going to do now? This calls for someone who can actually communicate with them.

I wait for a second, but unsurprisingly no translator comes diving at us.

I take a deep breath. *Okay, think.* They need to get down to their gate. There will probably be someone there who can help, but how can I get them there? The man has a walker, and I can't exactly give him a piggyback ride. But maybe if I take the woman with me, I can show her tickets to a gate agent and explain that they need assistance. Maybe find someone who speaks Tagalog.

Yes. That might work.

I point to the old man and then at a chair by the board. Then I gesture for the woman to go down the hall with me. The old man moves to follow us, and I point at the seat again and put my hand up like a stop sign. I'm not sure any of this miming is working, but the next thing I know, they say something to each other, the man sits, and the woman points down the corridor.

Wow. They did understand me.

We hustle along the hallway, and I feel bad about

making an old lady race-walk, but I don't want her to miss her flight.

When we finally get near the gate, I run up ahead. And it's busy. Really busy. Of course it is. The plane is boarding.

I scan around, looking for someone who can help, but all the gate agents are occupied. *Oh no.* I'm going to have to draw people's attention. I swallow hard. Then I look at the old lady. She nods at me, and I know what I have to do.

"Hey," I say. Two people turn. Not loud enough. I sigh and then draw all the air into my lungs that I can. "Hey!"

That makes a dozen people turn around.

"Sorry, but does anyone speak Tagalog?" I ask. I seriously don't know how my dads handle being loud and proud all the time when people stare at them. There's awkward quiet as people continue to gawk. And I kind of want to be anywhere else again, but I keep looking around.

Then, "I speak Tagalog," a boy says. He's around my age, I think.

Relief floods through me. "Thanks," I say.

I wave over the old woman. "I'm pretty sure she speaks Tagalog. Her husband has a walker and is waiting down at their old gate—E37. Can you tell her this is her new gate?"

"Oh. Um, yeah. Yeah, I will," he says. Then he starts speaking to the woman in Tagalog. And she smiles widely.

I stand there staring at the two of them. Happiness bubbles in my chest.

"I'll go ask someone to send a cart down to get her husband," the kid says to me.

The old lady pats my cheek gently and smiles. I smile back, then gesture that I'm going to go. She nods and smiles once more.

I take two steps, then turn back and see the boy talking to a gate attendant. They'll go pick up the old man, and the couple will make their flight.

And I'm glad. Really glad.

As I walk, I realize: I did it. I mean, I didn't suddenly become fluent in another language or start fist-fighting racists, but I managed to communicate, to help that couple.

And if I could get them to understand me even with a language barrier, maybe I could get my dads to understand, too.

Maybe.

When I reach Jamba, I stride up to Dads' table before I can lose my nerve and stand across from them.

"There you are," Daddy Brian says.

"You okay, Min? You were gone forever," Daddy Pat says.

"I'm okay." I sit down and stir my oatmeal, my nerve

dissolving like brown sugar in hot oats. I made it like thirty seconds. I sigh at myself. I guess it's different standing up to my dads instead of standing up for other people.

"So . . ." Daddy Brian clears his throat. "How are you, really?"

I stop stirring. *Put the spoon down and talk to them, Mindy.*

"Worried," I say.

"We've noticed. Is it about going back home?" Daddy Pat asks.

"No, it's . . ."

The words form inside me: It's not going back home. Home is a two-bedroom condo in Chelsea, Manhattan.

I may never be the kind of person who knows how to respond in the moment, but I was wrong before—that doesn't mean I'm a coward. I managed to help that couple. To speak up and ask for attention despite really, *really* not wanting to. My dads love me. They want to know what I'm thinking. I just need to tell them.

Even if it's not going to be what they want to hear.

I open my mouth.

"I don't like when you guys say things like that. Korea isn't home. I'm home here, even if I was born there."

I'm kind of shocked all of that came out of me. Dads look equally surprised.

Daddy Pat's blue eyes fill with concern, and he looks from Daddy Brian to me. "Oh, Min, I didn't mean to say that you're not home here. It's just that you were from there. I wasn't even born in Ireland, but I consider it my home in a way. I guess it's different for you, huh?"

I nod.

"Mindy, I'm sorry," he says. "I didn't mean to make you feel like you're not a part of us or from here, like that woman did. I'd never want to do that. But . . . I did. I'll do better."

He reaches his hand across, and I take it. With our fingers touching, I find the courage to say the rest of it.

"I just . . . I don't want to go. And I feel like you're both pushing too hard."

Daddy Brian tilts his head. "You don't want to go to Korea?"

"I don't know the culture, or have family there, or even speak the language. I don't have a connection to Korea—not really. I . . . I don't think I'm ready."

We all sit in the silence of that truth. They seem kind of stunned. Probably the whole I-didn't-say-anything-and-went-along-with-this-for-months-and-we're-in-an-airport-on-the-way thing.

"I kind of wish you'd brought this up earlier," Daddy Pat says.

"I . . . I didn't think you'd understand."

"We don't have to go if you really don't want to—if you're not ready, Min," Daddy Brian says.

I stare at both of them, my eyes feeling bulgy.

"What?" I yelp.

"You didn't hear the announcement?" Daddy Pat asks. "They just canceled the flight."

It must've happened when I was knocking people down in the other concourse. I lean back, stunned, but still holding on to Daddy Pat's hand.

"But what about all the other reservations?" I ask.

"We'll take care of it," Daddy Pat says. "That's what travel insurance is for."

Daddy Brian nods and extends his hand, too. "We wanted to do something good, but we should've asked. We would never want to force this trip on you."

I take his hand as my whole body relaxes. As we sit quietly, more cancellations are announced because of the storm. It all sinks in: we're not going. Not today, anyhow. "Maybe I'll feel different next year?" I say.

Daddy Pat shrugs. "You may. But it's okay if you don't. This time you tell us when you're feeling ready."

"After you finish eating, Min, we'll go to the ticket counter and arrange to go home," Daddy Pat says.

"Okay," I say.

I dig in. The oatmeal is a little cold, and the smoothie is a little warm, but it's the best meal I've had with my dads in a while.

Once I'm done, we stand and throw out our garbage. We pass where the woman and her son had gone by. I wish it hadn't taken all that for me to be able to talk to my dads. I wish I'd thought they'd understand before. But, as I take their hands again and we leave, I know that in the future I can. That I can stand up for me and sometimes even mime enough to stand up for other people, too.

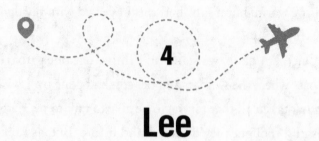

4

Lee

Uncle Jack started every video call the same way. "Hey, it's the best Asian guitarist in the world. And the *only* Asian guitarist in the world."

And every time, Lee would respond the same way.

First he would bite down on his lip to stop himself from rolling his eyes.

But then he'd laugh.

Because it was both funny and true. Maybe he wasn't the best in the *world*, but at least at the Berkeley School of Rock. He'd won the recent shred contest, a challenge among all the students to see who could play scales as fast as possible without a single wrong note. At twelve years old, he'd even beaten students older than him. That earned the title of "best." As for "only," well, "Lee Chang" was the only Asian name on the roster, so of course he won there.

In fact, he couldn't think of *any* Asian guitar players, let alone guitar gods. He'd almost searched once, just to see if Uncle Jack was right. But he decided he didn't want to know—didn't need to know.

Lee offered his usual joke reply to Uncle Jack: "I'm half-Asian."

Uncle Jack laughed, his head tilting back as the screen froze and pixelated. Lee squinted, the only movement from the selfie camera as the Wi-Fi strength dropped to two bars. He ran a hand through his chin-length dark brown hair, his selfie image doing the same. "Uncle Jack?"

". . . you'd . . . make it . . . fine?"

Airport Wi-Fi. Lee's mom had warned him about the way it was unreliable and slow, and besides, he had promised his parents he'd save his battery just in case any emergencies happen. This was the first time he was allowed to fly alone, and getting them to agree to Southwest's twelve-and-above policy had been hard enough. He really should keep his word. But he wanted to tell Uncle Jack the good news. Lee repeated "Can you hear me?" several times until Uncle Jack started moving again on the screen.

"There you are," Uncle Jack said, his words out of sync with his image. The sound clipped out with a buzz- ing noise, and Lee looked around to see if anyone in the food court noticed. Minutes ago, it'd been busy. But people had eaten their food or gotten their coffee or whatever, so at least for now, only pockets of travelers remained. Some standing in line, some sitting quietly, and most just staring at their phones. Although, a couple of security guards talked loudly enough to be heard.

"So, check this out," Lee said, pride pushing his cheeks into a wide grin. With one hand, he held his phone up to get the right angle. With the other, he reached over and flipped down the locks on his rectangular hard-shell guitar case. The lid refused to budge under his fingertips, and he said, "Hold on," complete with an exasperated sigh, before he unstuck it.

The lid finally opened to reveal a guitar. Not necessarily the best or most expensive guitar, but the most important guitar in the world.

Because it was *his*: a blue standard-model Stratocaster with a white pick guard, fresh strings changed out only a week ago. Next to it sat a small ziplock bag of guitar picks and the palm-sized, plug-in mini-amp that made it possible to jam anywhere—even if you could barely hear it.

"Ohhhh," Uncle Jack said, his voice louder than the sudden announcements from the airport PA system. "Nice. You got it through TSA?"

"Yeah. I just walked up and said, 'I have a musical instrument stored safely in a case.' They opened it, and that was it. Didn't even have to bring up the Modernization and Reform Act. They asked more about me traveling alone."

"Cool." Then Uncle Jack leaned into the camera. "You've been practicing?"

Lee knew what Uncle Jack meant. Not practicing riffs, but practicing *the* most monstrous riff of all time: "Eruption" by Van Halen.

Sure, it was decades old—Uncle Jack said it came out a few years before he was born in the early 1980s. But even though years and years of music had happened since then, nothing quite sounded like those two minutes of Eddie Van Halen shredding all over a fretboard.

Problem was, it was also one of the hardest songs in history to play. The fact that Lee actually got most of it was a bit of a miracle. The finger-tapping technique needed for the middle, well, his hands kept slipping during that part, no matter how many times he'd tried in the past few months. Sometimes he'd sit for an hour, trying that same thirty-second section over and over, until his palm was sweaty and his fingers raw. Other times, he'd pick up his guitar, give it one spontaneous try, then stop. Or he'd do something in between. It didn't matter, though, because the same thing happened every time. He told himself that the first step to becoming a guitar god had to be playing through that riff.

He wasn't quite there yet.

"Practicing. But my tapping still stinks. I actually got the last part down, though."

"Ha," Uncle Jack said with a bright grin. "I'll help you learn to tap. I've never been able to play the end, though. Can't play steady at that speed. So maybe *you* can teach *me*."

"You got it, Uncle Jack."

"Awesome, dude. We are going to have the best jam session when you get here. Protect your guitar with all your kung fu skills." On-screen, Uncle Jack swished his free tattooed arm around, fingers forming a fist.

Lee wanted to correct Uncle Jack, first to say that his knuckles should be lined up with his forearm when punching to avoid breaking his wrist, and second, he didn't have any magic kung fu knowledge. He'd only learned about the wrist thing when the school's karate club had a lunch demo. Why would Uncle Jack think he knew kung fu?

Lee shook his head, a strange weight in his gut, and though he felt like doing anything but smiling, he forced one out. And just to make Uncle Jack happy, up went a fist. In proper form.

"That's it," Uncle Jack said, his man-bun bobbing with a nod and freckled cheeks rising. "Come on, get pumped.

We're gonna jam. We're gonna go to a gig. It's going to be the best holiday weekend."

A yell came from down the airport hall, followed by the pound of footsteps. Lee shut his guitar case, then looked up from his table to see several security officers in blue shirts rushing past, the lead speaking into a walkie-talkie.

"You all right, kiddo?"

"Yeah." But something was definitely going on. Low voices started to murmur all around him, then shouts came from across the airport's large hall. One by one, people in the nearby waiting area stood up, craning their necks to see. "Actually, I think something weird is happening. Call you back in a bit."

"Cool deal." Uncle Jack stretched out the word "cool" like he always did, then smiled another toothy grin through his orange beard and waved before disappearing.

More security followed quickly. Lee watched as guards walked by with big steps and swinging arms. He stood up and slung his backpack over one shoulder, then moved away from his table, trying to listen in on what they were talking about. "Uh-huh . . . uh-huh . . . copy that," the man in front said into the walkie-talkie before stopping and yelling back to the two people behind him. "Sweep the area, collect any loose objects."

The officers spread out, the lead one walking past Lee's view. Lee took several steps over to look through the food court's entrance. In every direction, others also watched, drawn out of their seats by whatever this commotion was. The lead officer had stopped in front of the bookstore, talking with the sales clerk while pointing in every direction. Lee leaned forward, trying to make out any details of their conversation.

But after a minute, the man simply moved on, and the other security officers disappeared into the bustling airport. Without them to watch, people returned to their phones and books.

Lee exhaled and shook his head. "Loose objects," he muttered to himself, and then turned, surprised that he'd stepped a little farther than he'd meant to from the table. He checked the time on his phone and called Uncle Jack back—then realized that the two security guards who had been eating in the food court had also moved.

Now they lurked by the garbage can several tables away, arms crossed over their blue shirts.

And they were looking at his guitar case.

"Loose objects," he repeated to himself, though with a totally different meaning this time. The burly men stood, both with the reddish tint that white people got from too much sun, and they talked quietly to each other. Then one spoke into his walkie-talkie while the other grinned.

"Everything okay?" Uncle Jack asked as soon as the connection was made, but Lee ignored him. "Lee? Lee? Hey, dude, what's wrong?"

Rather than answer Uncle Jack, Lee hit the End Call button with his thumb and slid back into his chair, tossing his backpack down by his feet. He grabbed a few curly fries and then pulled out his phone again, loading up *Tetris* and trying to look as casual as possible.

Almost a minute passed, but the security guards stuck around. He thought he heard one snicker, but he couldn't be sure; Lee didn't want to turn his head and give away that he was trying to monitor *their* monitoring. Instead, he played *Tetris* on autopilot, doing his best to look busy while feeling the weight of their stares.

They watched him. But why?

Tetris blocks piled up on-screen, his movements too sloppy to form any lines. The screen flashed, the game asked if he wanted to start over, and Lee made a decision.

He reached over and pulled his guitar case close to him.

"Excuse me, son," one of the security guards said, stepping nearer. The word "son" sounded the complete opposite of how it did when Lee's Midwest grandpa gently said it.

Lee had never encountered police or security before, outside of a school presentation or saying "hello" or "thank you."

He did, however, know exactly what this tone meant. Every jerk cop in every movie ever made talked like this.

Lee snuck a peek at the pair of frowning uniformed men looking at him, then locked his eyes on the guitar case.

The taller security guard cleared his throat and repeated himself. "Excuse me, son."

"Oh, hi . . ." What word should he use? Sir? Officer? Nothing at all? "Hi, officers. This is mine." There. Clean and simple and confident.

And honest. Nothing to judge. He was just a kid eating lunch, on his way to see his uncle. With his legally approved guitar.

The bald man on the left—KOWLER etched on his name tag—pointed at the instrument case. "What's that?" he asked, his salt-and-pepper goatee lifting up when his mouth curled.

"It's a guitar."

"Hmm," the other guard said. He stood several inches shorter than Kowler, though with a trimmer physique. The name UMBRIDGE was etched on the name tag on his broad chest. "Far too big for a carry-on. Seems awfully suspicious."

"No, no," Lee said, but then he caught himself. Was he being defiant? Or rude? Would that make things worse? "It's just a guitar."

"Listen, kid," Kowler said. "I don't think you realize this, but the airport's in a bit of a situation here. So, it would really help if you weren't trying to slow us down."

"No, look, it's totally legal." Suddenly, all the notes Uncle Jack sent him came in extra handy. "You're allowed to bring on musical instruments. The FAA Modernization and Reform Act of 2012 says so, as long as there's room. And I upgraded my boarding slot to make sure there would be plenty of space so—"

"Where are your parents?"

"I'm flying by myself," Lee said, the words making him naturally feel bigger. "Lemme open it and I'll show you—it's a blue Stratocaster."

He moved to click open the case's locks when an "Ah ah ah" interrupted him. "Don't do that. Don't touch anything," Kowler said before motioning Umbridge back several steps. Lee glanced around the food court, the various cooks and cashiers working like nothing extraordinary was happening. Same with the people sitting; most looked at their phones, and only one older woman gave him a second glance.

He felt the officers' eyes as they continued speaking

to each other, Umbridge with his thumbs hanging on his belt and Kowler rubbing his goatee with arms crossed, and though they talked quietly, the words came through clear enough for Lee to hear. "I don't know. Still seems pretty suspicious."

"You think?" Umbridge asked. He tilted his chin, an overhead light reflecting off his rough cheeks.

"Look at him. There's no way he plays guitar." Lee's gut twisted at that sentence. How could they say that? He was even wearing a Ramones shirt. They were *the* punk band. Should he explain how Uncle Jack introduced him to classic punk? "Maybe piano," Kowler added. "Or, like, violin. But not guitar."

Lee knew *exactly* what that meant.

Because there were no Asian guitar gods. Classical musicians like Yo-Yo Ma and his cello, sure, but rock stars? Nope.

"Ah," Umbridge said, his lips sticking out as he nodded. "See what you mean. But that T-shirt. That's a legit band."

"Right. But they sell bootleg shirts in Chinatown."

Thoughts whirled through Lee's head. He could talk about bands. And how his parents weren't like other parents, how they got him into music—real music, not just the popular stuff. How they lived in Berkeley, where his mom—Uncle Jack's sister—worked as an illustrator, and his dad taught philosophy at UC Berkeley. He wasn't like what the officers were talking about. He played rock guitar, not piano or violin. He'd always stood apart, except at School of Rock, where he fit right in—just like he wanted. "This isn't a bootleg," he said. "I got it from their website."

"Sure you did, kid."

Their walkie-talkies squawked in unison, Kowler answering, a muffled voice saying something about an all clear, though the details were drowned out. "Understood," he said into the walkie before looking at Lee. "What's your name?"

"Lee Chang. C-H-A-N-G," he said, adding the spelling like he always did.

"Well, Lee Chang," the guard said, patting the guitar case, "this is a suspicious object. We gotta take it in." Umbridge stepped forward, and though he seemed like a pretty average adult height, Lee felt like he, himself, had somehow shrunk down to the size of a guitar pick. "You have to understand, you don't look like someone who plays guitar. I mean, come on."

Inside Lee, everything electrified: his thoughts, his muscles, his heart.

Suddenly, every second he had ever put into practicing the guitar, every layer of calluses on his fingertips, all led to this moment. In the food court at Chicago Gateway International Airport.

"Let me show you," he said. In one motion, Lee clicked open the guitar case, threw back the top, and slung his Stratocaster over his shoulder. He plugged the mini-amp into the guitar's output jack and turned it up as loud as the tiny speaker would go.

Then Lee stood up, like a guitar god about to take the stage.

Except here, he stood on his chair at a food court. But he felt every eye on him, from the guards to the cashiers.

He fished a guitar pick from his pocket, then held it between his fingers.

There was only one thing to do, one song to play.

Lee slammed the opening A5 chord of "Eruption" and began the riff that started low, then walked up high, before screaming back down low. Then *boom-boom-boom*, three power chords in a row. The fingers of his left hand flew up the fretboard, sliding the high string up for rapid-fire playing, and shredding at full speed as notes flew out of the mini-amp. Sweat formed on his temple, but he didn't care; his head bobbed, fingers spider-walking down the fretboard to finish the section.

The notes rang out, a chain-saw-like buzz that wobbled with his whammy bar.

All around him, heads turned and murmurs started. He couldn't hear what they said, but he knew they watched. And listened.

He went into the next riff, moving up the middle strings at full speed, his heart pounding in time. Because this was the next section, the part he never got right—the part where his hands always slipped.

The finger tapping.

He started, his left hand on the frets and his right hand moving close, a special technique only for the fastest of metal guitar. And with the weight of an audience watching him, he closed his eyes and locked in, his fingers answering. In perfect time. He didn't think about it, an entire wall of sound coming out rapid-fire. And the strangest thing happened:

His hand didn't slip.

In fact, he'd gotten through the whole section, the first time he'd ever done that, from the triumphant peak of arpeggiated high notes to the walk down before he slid a dive-bomb on the low string, the note ringing out while he leaned on the whammy bar; then he fired off a quick power chord to close it out.

The final roar faded, the sound from the mini-amp

gradually absorbing into the noise of the airport, and he breathed hard, like he'd just sprinted for two straight minutes. Which he kind of had, except with his fingers.

He looked up to see everyone in the food court staring at him. Maybe because of the wild guitar playing. But also maybe because he was standing on his chair.

"What was that?" Kowler asked with a laugh.

"Um," Lee said, the question stealing anything good he felt. "'Eruption' by Van Halen?"

"Sounded like a bunch of buzzing to me," Umbridge said. "Where'd you get that toy amp?"

"It's a practice amp."

"Uh-huh. Does it work with your violin?"

Violin? He'd just played "Eruption" flawlessly.

"Eruption" wasn't only difficult, the song was on the level of guitar gods. And they didn't care. They laughed.

In that moment, even though everything looked and sounded and felt the same as the second prior, the world became different.

Lee bit down on his lip. He'd tried. He'd tried *so* hard to be a rock musician. And he knew what that violin comment meant. Was it so difficult to believe an Asian kid could shred like Eddie Van Halen?

"Ugh," he let out without thinking.

The men turned to him.

He hadn't meant to say that. To recover, he coughed. Then cleared his throat. Anything to get away from the situation, to let him melt into the background. All he wanted was to go visit Uncle Jack—why were they giving him such *grief*?

"Something you want to say to us?"

"I'm . . ." Behind him, people passed, a combination of voices and footsteps and rolling suitcases, totally ignoring what was happening. "It's just my guitar," he finally said, his voice quiet. "I'm going to visit my uncle. We're going to have a jam session. He plays in bands. He's going to take me to a show. Look." Lee pulled out his phone and loaded up a picture of Uncle Jack's band. "He's the rhythm guitarist." He held up the screen, half expecting the officers to take his phone as well for no reason. "He's the one who told me how to get through TSA. He said musical instruments have special exemptions."

"Now you're really stretching it. He doesn't look like a Chang."

"He's my mom's brother," Lee spit out, the words escaping simply because he felt too tired to keep them in.

"Oh." Kowler and Umbridge looked at each other again, Umbridge giving a shrug. "Oh, I get it now," Umbridge said before leaning over, inspecting the guitar that still hung off Lee's shoulders.

Kowler tapped the plug-in mini-amp with his finger-nail. "Just a guitar," Kowler said, then plucked the top string, the low open E note barely ringing out over the sound of the food court, and as he did, all the air escaped Lee's lungs, the release of tension leaving him slightly dizzy. "Guess it's yours."

"Huh," Umbridge said. "I'm surprised. Could have sworn there'd be a violin in there."

"Maybe it's a half guitar, half violin."

Their walkie-talkies squawked in unison. "Okay, break time's over," Kowler said. *Break time?* Didn't they just say his guitar was suspicious? "Copy that, this is five-oh-seven, we're close by, and we'll go check it out."

"We're just messing with you, kid," Umbridge said. "Got you pretty good. Go see your uncle." He plucked the E string again, then stepped back. "Lighten up. You're not bad."

Not bad. So they did hear everything. They saw him play it all, without a single mistake, and they turned it into a big joke. What was Lee supposed to do? Be calm and say nothing? Be grateful? Be polite?

He'd just played "Eruption," which was, like, impossible. He'd *earned* the right to be cool.

"Yeah," he said, fingers forming to hold a power chord. He ran the pick through the strings. "I'll make sure to rock." The instant the words left his mouth, Lee's cheeks burned. "I'll make sure to rock" was a terrible choice, not cool at all. It was what someone might say if they were really a huge dork but *wanted* to seem cool.

The officers looked at each other, smirks on their faces, then started to walk away, past the food court entrance and into the main hall. But he heard what Kowler said: "Wow, an Asian kid who plays guitar. That's new. Is he like the only one?"

● ● ●

Four minutes is the average length of a rock song.

Here, four minutes had passed since the guards left. One song.

Four minutes that felt like forty or four hundred. But it still meant that Lee had an hour before boarding. He picked at his lunch, though his hunger was gone, then he cleared his table without eating any more of it. Instead, his mind was stuck on what had just happened. The officers were only "messing" with him? But why? Why would they do that? Even if they were joking around, how could they miss that the sheer difficulty of what he'd played touched upon the realm of guitar gods?

Except they were right. No guitar gods were Asian.

And maybe that meant Lee could never be one, either.

Across the way, Lee found an open chair in front of an

empty gate. He settled, putting his backpack down first, then his guitar. The heel of his shoe pressed against the hard shell of the case, a constant reminder that it was still there.

Then he called Uncle Jack back.

"Hey, it's the best Asian guitarist in the world. And the *only* Asian—"

"Hey, Uncle Jack," Lee said, cutting the joke off.

"You okay?" Lines of concern crinkled across Uncle Jack's brow. "What happened?"

"There's some security thing going on here. Some people . . ." Lee paused, then left it at, "Some people were being jerks about it."

"To you?" Uncle Jack's look of concern deepened. Lee couldn't respond, though Uncle Jack must have seen an answer in his silence. "Hey, dude. Look. There are some not-cool people out there. Really terrible. Don't let them get to you. Shake it off. You got your mini-amp with you?"

"Yeah."

"Just practice for a bit, think about something else. You want me to show you tapping technique really quick?"

"Actually," Lee started before pausing. Should he tell Uncle Jack about how he'd played "Eruption"?

No. Not right now. It didn't matter.

"I think I got it," Lee said. "But maybe I'll practice before we take off."

Uncle Jack grinned behind the fuzz of his beard. "Sounds good. Save your battery for emergencies." Lee's mom must have talked to him. "I'll see you in a few hours. We'll jam. It's gonna be awesome."

Uncle Jack disappeared, leaving Lee to stare as the screen changed from the call log to his home screen of a vertical fretboard. After thirty seconds, it dimmed to half brightness before disappearing completely, only his reflection staring back.

Asian eyes. Asian skin. Asian hair.

That was what people saw. Not the guitar, not the player. Even if he could rock the most difficult song of all time.

Why should he even bother if no one ever saw him as a guitarist?

Lee's phone buzzed, announcing a text from Uncle Jack with a link. He clicked it to load up an article about Eddie Van Halen's tapping technique. Uncle Jack must have sent it as his way of helping.

But then Lee saw the most unexpected headline in the related posts on the side of the article: *Eddie Van Halen and family endured "horrifying racism" growing up.*

His finger trembled as he tapped the link.

It was a profile about Eddie Van Halen posted shortly after the rock legend's death that described the "second-class citizen" status his Indonesian mother faced and the awful things he'd dealt with as a kid because of who he was—torn-up homework, eating sand, and all sorts of other playground terrors.

Lee sat back in his chair, reading and rereading paragraphs.

Eddie Van Halen's dad was Dutch, and his mom was *Indonesian*.

The greatest guitar player in rock history was part Asian.

Like him.

Ignoring his mom's request to save battery, he decided right then and there to deep-dive for "Asian guitarists," and he clicked on an article with a list of names: James Iha. Mike Shinoda. Kim Thayil. Kirk Hammett was half-Asian, Karen O and KT Tunstall as well.

He stared at the list, and while he didn't know all their music, just seeing their names made the world change again. How had he not known about them? He felt a flash of anger at himself for having never dared to look before. But no, he told himself. He shouldn't be mad about something that barely anyone knew. Instead, he should be mad at the officers and others—even Uncle Jack—for thinking they could joke about this. *They* should know better.

Lee looked at the clock and figured he still had about fifty minutes until boarding. With his foot, he scooted out his guitar case and snapped open the locks. He grabbed his most prized possession and strummed, then plugged in his mini-amp.

There weren't many guitarists like him. But that could change.

Someday, someone with his eyes, his skin, his hair would step out onstage, hear the screams, and hit the opening riff of the biggest song in the world.

If someone, then why not him?

He could be the one to change it.

After all, he'd nailed "Eruption." Not even Uncle Jack could pull that off.

The thought sank in as Lee plucked at the strings, moving his fingers over the fretboard just like Eddie Van Halen.

A voice caught Lee's attention, and he looked up. Two girls looked back at him, one about his age, and one probably in kindergarten or first grade. The younger one's eyes were wide, and Lee wondered if she'd ever seen a guitar in real life before—or anyone like *him* playing a guitar. Lee played a short blues riff and offered a quick smile.

The older girl returned a thoughtful look, while her younger sister kept beaming, and they locked in for several seconds before the two turned and left, the younger one skipping away.

They disappeared from view, and Lee played a chord, letting the strings ring out. As he sat, he knew something had to be different when his flight landed.

When Uncle Jack picked him up, Lee would do two things. First he'd play "Eruption" for him.

And then he'd tell him that he didn't want to hear that joke anymore—and why that joke *wasn't* cool.

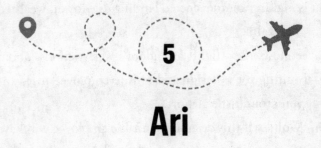

Ari

Rules for Traveling as an Unaccompanied Minor with
Your Six-Year-Old Brother
A Work in Progress, by Ari Cheung, age 12

General rules for the plane:

1. Don't let Ezzie eat cookies. Six-year-olds + sugar = TROUBLE.
2. If a flight attendant gives you cookies, and you can't stop Ezzie before he eats them, don't let him have any more cookies.
3. If other passengers give Ezzie their cookies, pretend to be asleep and hope the sugar high wears off by the time you reach California.

What to do when the captain announces that your nonstop flight is making an unexpected landing due to bad weather:

1. Stay calm.
2. Follow the flight attendant's instructions about waiting for a designated airline employee to escort you around the airport.
3. Wonder if this designated airline employee will have more sparkly unicorn stickers, because Ezzie has already used up the stickers in his Designated Sibling Preparedness Pack (© Ari Cheung).
4. Wish you'd been better at reminding Ezzie that the stickers were for his activity book, not his face, head, hands, shirt, and/or shoes.
5. Hope that Nainai has a good method of getting stickers out of hair. Make a note to ask her as soon as you get to San Diego.

As the plane lands and you calm down Ezzie, who heard "unexpected landing" and jumped to "emergency," you reflect on how you got in this situation in the first place:

1. Mom and Dad got divorced last year.
2. Since the divorce, you've been watching Ezzie A LOT.
3. Mom and Dad promised that if you're responsible this summer, and take good care of Ezzie, they'll let you go on the Quiz Bowl trip next year (a HUGE deal!).

4. Hence the record you're keeping of your babysitting decisions, plus tips and tricks for any other older siblings who need them. You're proactive that way.

Things your six-year-old brother should NOT say in a loud voice when your plane lands due to bad weather:
1. MAYDAY
2. I FEEL SICK.
3. More cookies?
4. WHEEEEEEE!

Things you observe when you get off at the Chicago airport:
1. Joan is your designated airline employee.
2. Joan does not look very happy about it.
3. Probably because Joan did not sign up to babysit two strange kids for who knows how long.
4. You sympathize with Joan. You also did not sign up to shepherd a six-year-old from parent to parent. It just sort of worked out that way.
5. Remind yourself about the Quiz Bowl trip and take a deep breath. Time to be EXTRA responsible.
6. Pause to admire a girl in a purple NYU sweatshirt with two long braids and a face that's full of determination. Wish you had an ounce of that confidence. Focus when you realize Ezzie is touching

every surface you pass. This calls for ALL the hand sanitizer—luckily a staple of the Designated Sibling Preparedness Pack (© Ari Cheung).

Texts you get when your direct flight has to make an unexpected landing due to weather, for who knows how long:

1. Mom: OMG RU OK?!!
2. Dad: Who can I call?! Are you with an airline employee?!
3. Nainai: Ari, Please text me so I know you are safe. Love, Nainai
4. Jenny (best friend): You're stranded at an airport? SO COOL!
5. Mom: 🍕?
6. Dad: Have you eaten?
7. Nainai: Ari, Be sure to get something to eat. Love, Nainai
8. Mom: Including vegetables
9. Dad: Don't let Ezzie have sugar
10. Nainai: Ari, Be sure to get dessert. Treat yourself. Love, Nainai

(Sidenote: Nainai learned "treat yourself" from the internet—it's her new favorite phrase.)

The journey from the gate to the food court is:

1. FAR. Who designed airports—angry gym teachers?

2. Crowded. The air is full of people whose flights are grounded or delayed, and they are CRANKY and frantic. You watch a boy about your age running behind his parents as they hurry him along. He's clutching a book and looks dazed, like he just woke up. You sympathize and hope there will be no running in your future.

3. Full of juggling. Joan takes Ezzie's rolling pink unicorn bag, which is nice of her. But Ezzie insists on holding his Designated Sibling Preparedness Pack in his hand, which means you have his stuffed lizard and coloring set, on top of your own suitcase and backpack, which is HEAVY. (Which is also why you're hoping there will be ZERO running involved in this airport experience.)

4. You stop for a second and put Ezzie's toys in your backpack. You take out the three big books you have in there to carry in your arms, to make the pack lighter.

5. "What are those?" Joan asks when you resume, looking at the books with a puzzled frown.

6. "Hebrew School homework," you say. "For my Bat Mitzvah."

7. Joan looks confused.

8. "We're Jewish," you say.

Common reactions when you tell people that you're Jewish:

1. "WHAT?! YOU'RE JEWISH? HOW IS THAT POSSIBLE?!" (Said in a tone that implies that you are a unicorn, or other mythical creature.)

2. "*You're* Jewish? Really? Prove it. Say a prayer." (Said in a tone that implies they expect you to follow this command and "prove yourself" to them, like they set the bar for all things Jewish.)

3. Wait, are you *real* Jewish? (Said in a tone that implies you can be "unreal" Jewish, which is weird, because it's a religion, and you can celebrate your religion however you want—it's personal, as Rabbi Chaya says.)

Back to Joan:

1. Joan goes for number one.

2. "You're Jewish?!" She looks at your face for signs that you're kidding. "How did that happen?!"

Review strategies for answering:

1. Yes, Judaism is a diverse, global religion. There are Jewish populations all around the world, not to mention the fact that in an increasingly diverse America, interracial and interfaith marriages happen all the time. . . . (Dad's answer: he loves facts.)

2. Well, when two people love each other very, very much, and one is Chinese and one is Jewish, they decide to have a baby. . . . (Mom's answer: she's sick of the question and likes to mess with people.)

3. Yes. My mom is Jewish, my dad is Chinese. (My answer: easy, to the point, answers the question with minimal effort.)

Steps for navigating the exchange that follows:

1. Opt for number three, say: "Yes. My mom is Jewish, and my dad is Chinese."

2. Keep your face neutral as Joan says: "Wow. How unusual."

3. Nod vaguely, like you are neither agreeing nor disagreeing.

4. File this conversation away for when you explain to Rabbi Chaya that you really aren't sure about this whole Bat Mitzvah thing.

Things you have to do when having a Bat Mitzvah:

1. Stand at the bimah, which means you're in front of EVERYONE, almost like you're on a stage.

2. Read from the Torah, in Hebrew, as well as all the prayers that go along with it.

3. Give a speech about your Torah reading and what it means to you.

4. Make a commitment to being a part of the larger Jewish community.

Reasons you don't think you want a Bat Mitzvah:

1. Because the Chinese side of your family won't know what's going on.

2. Because public speaking, period.

3. And not to mention the principle of the thing. Rabbi Chaya says that a Bat Mitzvah is when you stand up as a member of your world—when you take part in your larger community. She likes to talk about the Hebrew word "hineni." It means "Here I am." Rabbi Chaya says we say "hineni" every time we stand up for who we are, or stand for what's right, or stand by someone else because they need justice.

Rabbi Chaya is pretty cool, no lie.

She wants you to include all of your family in the Bat Mitzvah. She says that's what a Bat Mitzvah is for: when you celebrate all parts of yourself and say, "I'm here, I'm ready, I'm one of you."

4. But are you?

5. Joan looks at you, and the first thing she thinks is

"How unusual." And do you know who else thinks you're "unusual" and "weird"?

   a.   Other Jewish kids.

   b.   Parents in the synagogue.

   c.   Hebrew School teachers, who always get a little confused by what you're doing there.

   d.   Literally everyone who finds out you're Jewish.

6.   And the thing is, it also happens with the other side of your family. When you're in Chinatown, you know people give you looks. They don't realize that you're related to Nainai and Yeye until someone explains it to them. They don't think you can use chopsticks. And they also get confused when you say you're Jewish.

7.   And you're tired of always having to explain.

8.   In fact, sometimes, when you're in either place— whether it's Hebrew School or Chinatown—it's hard to really be there. You're so in your head, wondering what other people think.

9.   So maybe a Bat Mitzvah is not for you. Maybe this is a message that you're whatever the opposite of hineni is.

10.   Not here. Not ready. Not really a part of anything.

You have to focus because the food court is:

1.   PACKED.

You wait in line:

1. FOR FOREVER.
2. While you wait, Joan asks: "So why are you headed to San Diego?"
3. You explain: "To visit our dad."
4. Ezzie explains: "Because of divawce!"

Reasons why Mom and Dad divorced:

1. They were SO patently bad for each other and fought all the time.
2. Dad got a new job on the West Coast.

That's actually about it.

When people hear about this, the most commonly asked question is: "Are you sad that your parents divorced?" The answers are unexpected:

1. Weirdly, it's kind of a relief. They're both so much happier, and now that they aren't married, they seem to be actual friends, which is nice. They're still a team, which means you can't get away with double allowances or pretending your bedtime is eleven with Mom, so Dad should let you stay up later. Which is less nice. But, overall, it's fine.
2. But the thing you don't like is that everything is so separate. You were already juggling between two very

different sides of the family when your parents were together. Now it's like two different worlds. There's one world with Mom and her rules, and Bubbe and Zayde, and Passover seders, and old-movie nights. And then there's Dad with his world, and Nainai and Yeye, and trips to Chinatown, and rice soup for breakfast every morning (which is DELICIOUS, by the way). And each world is like a different planet now that they're literally in two different places. It's a strange feeling. That's why the thought of them all in one room next summer, at your Bat Mitzvah, feels like an extra NO. These two worlds are different enough and hard enough as it is, without adding public speaking and TONS of Hebrew that you're sure to mess up anyway. Let's not complicate things further.

You finally order, and then Joan takes Ezzie to find a table while you:

1. Wait for your Smashburgers and put your Hebrew School books back in your backpack so no one else can see them.
2. Think about what you'll say to convince Rabbi Chaya that this whole Bat Mitzvah thing should be put off.
3. Get your food, and make sure to get plenty of napkins, because Ezzie.

The table is:

1. Small.
2. Surrounded by chairs made of tight-knit wire mesh, with little holes in them.
3. Now full of Ezzie's coloring books.

You:

1. Clear room.
2. Look away for ONE SECOND, YOU SWEAR, just ONE.
3. Look back and kiss the Quiz Bowl trip goodbye.

Steps for dealing with a brother crisis:

1. DO NOT PANIC.
2. Assess the situation calmly, and ask: "WHY DID YOU PUT YOUR FINGER IN THERE, EZZIE?!!!!!!"
3. Try not to scream in frustration when he says matter-of-factly, "I wanted to see if it would fit." His finger is jammed in the tiny grid of one of the chairs. "And it did!" he declares. "Just on the way in, not on the way out."
4. Try to pull Ezzie's finger out. It will not come out.
5. Look at Joan, who tries using some of her expensive hand cream to slip Ezzie's finger out. (Which is nice

of her.) The cream smells good but dries too quickly, and the finger doesn't budge.

6. Try to pick up the chair and see if Ezzie's finger will come out if the chair is upside down (it does not), while Joan goes to the bathroom for hand soap.

7. Try not to notice when people begin looking over at you.

Some ABSURD things that happen when your little brother has caused a major problem in a packed food court:

1. A few nice adults come over to help and offer suggestions.

2. You wish they would go away. Now you're drawing even more attention.

3. None of their suggestions work.

4. Joan comes back with the soap. It's the gross kind of soap that manages to be foamy and watery all at once. That doesn't work, either.

5. By now, you can DEFINITELY hear people in the food court talking about you.

6. A couple waiting for a table wonders jokingly if they can have yours while everyone is busy with the chair.

7. Wish you were NOT here.

8. Especially when a security guard comes to help. "We may have to cut it out of the chair," she says. "I'll call maintenance and see if they have any bolt cutters."

Just when things can't get any worse:

1. An announcement comes over the airport PA system. "Attention, passengers. Flight 363 to San Diego will be reboarding in thirty minutes. Please make your way to the gate. . . ."
2. "That's us!" Ezzie says. He looks at me, worried. Suddenly, he realizes how bad this is. He is about to cry.
3. You close your eyes. This CANNOT be happening.

But it is. And as Joan and the security guard bustle around you, trying to calm Ezzie, you hear:

1. "This is why children shouldn't be flying alone," a man's voice says. It's the couple from before. They've found a place to sit a few tables away. They're talking loudly, looking at you and Ezzie.
2. "Well, their parents don't know any better," the woman says. "Cultural differences and all that."
3. Even Joan's head snaps up in their direction at that.
4. "Oh, careful," the man says in a joking way. "You'll offend someone."

5. "Well, if the parents were here, I'd give them a piece of my mind," the woman says. "Airports are bad enough as it is. . . ." She takes a long sip of her drink. "Ah. Is there anything better than tea?" she muses, changing the subject.

For a moment, you imagine two versions of the world:
1. You, in a movie version of your life:
   Walk over and say something EPIC. Probably something along the lines of: "WHAT IS WRONG WITH YOU?! You see a kid in trouble and that's your response? If my parents were here, you'd be SORRY."
2. You, in real life (as always):
   Turn away, pretend you didn't hear. It's not worth it. What would you even say?

At that moment:
1. Ezzie is wailing.
2. You realize that you are the worst big sister in the history of ever.
3. You also realize that your chances of going to Quiz Bowl nationals are now so remote, they might as well be in outer space.

4. And that when your parents find out about this, you will NEVER hear the end of it.
5. Especially because you might miss your flight, since the security guard is on the radio with maintenance, and it will be a while before they can get here.

In despair, you:
1. Give up. There's no solution and no way you can help.

Then, suddenly:
1. You lock eyes, across the food court, with someone who reminds you of Nainai.
2. She's working at one of the stalls selling Asian fusion food.
3. She looks at you and smiles.
4. It's a smile of knowing. Of welcome.
5. And suddenly, you know what to do.
6. You race over.
7. "Hey wait!" Joan calls, spinning away from her talk with the security guard as if to say, *I can't lose this one, too!*
8. "Be right back!" you call.
9. Because you have a plan. You are ready.

And the secret ingredient is . . .

1. Sesame oil! You've cooked with it with Dad and Nainai so many times. It's delicious and thick and slippery and PERFECT.
2. Ezzie's finger pops out with a *thunk* from between the metal grates.
3. His poor finger is pink and a little swollen, but otherwise okay.
4. Joan and the security guard cheer and applaud.
5. If Nainai were here, she'd fuss over Ezzie's finger until you rolled your eyes.
6. Now you fuss over it until Ezzie rolls his eyes.
7. "I'm fine!" he says. "It was an adwenture!"
8. You are more relieved than you have been in the entire history of ever.
9. You give Cynthia, your new friend from the food stall, a hug.
10. She hugs you back.

Steps for doing something you've never done before:

1. Collect your trash to throw away, instruct Ezzie NOT TO MOVE OR TOUCH ANYTHING.
2. Take your trash to the trash can that isn't closest to you but is closest to the couple sipping their airport tea.

3. Pause in front of the trash can, staring at them, until they notice you.

4. Declaim in your loudest, crispest, most factually informed Quiz Bowl voice: "Did you know that tea originated in China, probably more than six thousand years ago? So, every time you drink tea, just remember: it was brought to you by 'cultural differences.' You're welcome."

5. Drop the garbage loudly in the trash, still staring at them. Imagine you are dropping the mic, because you are.

6. Walk away from their stunned, silent faces.

7. Smile to yourself.

8. Stop smiling when you realize that Rabbi Chaya was right all along, because maybe you are ready for your Bat Mitzvah. Because you just stood up for something. For yourself. Your whole self. And you'd do it again, or for someone who needs it, in a heartbeat.

9. Smile again, because fine, Rabbi Chaya knows, like, one thing. Whatever. Yes, it felt good.

10. Rejoin the table as Joan helps Ezzie slip his unicorn backpack on.

11. Text Nainai: Will you help me choose my Bat Mitzvah

outfit? I was thinking I could wear a qipao. Could I borrow one of yours?

Steps for leaving the food court:

1. Help Ezzie gather his things.
2. Ignore the tea-drinking couple as you leave, though Joan looks at them curiously, like she's just noticed something.
3. Get a text from your mom: Why did Nainai just call and ask for pics of your Tallis? She says it has to go with ur dress? & she's going to buy u matching shoes?
4. Grin.
5. Be surprised that Joan is smiling at you. "Good news?" she asks. "Yeah," you say. "Planning for my Bat Mitzvah."
6. "That's great," Joan says. Her smile is still there, is genuine.
7. Feel your heart stop when Ezzie, passing by another chair, asks, "Ari, want to see how I got my finger stuck?"
8. Giggle when everyone at the tables around you also yells, "NO!!!!!"
9. Wave goodbye to the (mostly) helpful food court as you leave.

10. Ask Ezzie, "Hey, want to help me with my flash cards on the plane? I guess I'm having a Bat Mitzvah next summer, and I could really use your help."

11. Match Ezzie's excitement when he jumps up and down and says, "YES. Flash cawds!"

12. Walk toward the food court exit, following Joan.

13. Notice that Joan looks thoughtful. Maybe it's about something else, something totally unrelated. But maybe it's about those people with the tea. Maybe it's a seed. Who knows what ideas will blossom from it someday?

14. As you go, pass a girl in the food court. She's Asian American and wearing a big red bow that you wish you had, and a face mask. She looks uncertain, like she's walking toward something she's not too excited about.

15. Catch her eye and smile. Her eyes seem to smile back. Because in this moment you see each other. You have each other. You hope that wherever she's going, everything will be okay.

16. Reach out your hand. "Ezzie?" you ask.

17. "Here I am," he replies, slipping a tiny hand into yours, still smelling like soap and sesame oil.

18. Be surprised, because you're excited for the trip and the summer that's ahead. You can't wait to see

everyone. And that excitement builds and bubbles as you make your way through the crowd, toward your flight, toward your family, toward traditions old and new, and chaos and rules and facts you know and will learn. In this moment, stand tall and proud, knowing that you are here.

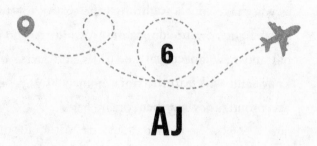

6

AJ

AJ's mind was the opposite of a highlight reel. As he stood in the long line for pizza, it replayed all his mistakes from the game last weekend. The airport's food court was packed due to weather delays, and a bunch of people had missed their flights, including his team, giving AJ's brain even more time to screen his failures:

There was that wide-open fast break where he lost his dribble and kicked the ball out of bounds.

His shot from the corner that got stuck *behind* the backboard.

The two free throws he bricked in the final minute that could have tied it up.

To name a few.

He had put up decent numbers. Hit a couple three-pointers. Threaded several bounce passes through the defenders crowding the lane. But from the moment the final buzzer blared, and his team's first loss of the season went into the books, his mind's eye showed only his mistakes over and over and over again.

If Saul had shown up to the game, AJ would've spent most of his time riding the bench like usual. But Saul hadn't—just like how he hadn't shown up at the airport this morning, either. So now AJ was on his way with the team to Vancouver for their big international tournament, so he could screw up in front of people from a bunch of other countries.

Thanks again for leaving me hanging, AJ texted Saul.

Saul replied with the upside-down smiley-face emoji.

Jk, AJ said. I know it's out of your control.

"Yo, kid," a teenager behind AJ said. "Move up."

AJ pulled his attention away from his phone and back into the crowded area buzzing with frustrated travelers weighed down by backpacks and bags. The line had moved forward. "Sorry," he mumbled, and closed the gap.

There had been a family in front of him, but they were gone now. They must have given up on the line, which was so long the scent of pizza barely reached AJ. Unfortunately, the family's departure meant that AJ now found himself directly behind his two least favorite teammates: Erik and Derek.

Gah, I'm stuck next to Tweedledee and Tweedledum in this pizza line, he updated Saul. *Is it worth it?*

Saul replied, *Depends—how hungry are you?*

VERY.

Erik and Derek played in the post, so they were taller and more muscular than AJ. They both had patchy facial hair and were the kind of bros who were almost always wearing AirPods. A stranger seeing AJ next to them would probably assume AJ was their little brother instead of their teammate, if not for the fact that all three of them wore matching red-and-white warm-ups embroidered with the *Perez, DDS* basketball logo. Derek's dad's dental practice had paid for the team's uniforms and warm-ups, and therefore gave the team its uninspired name: the Perez, DDS Chompers.

Neither Erik nor Derek noticed that AJ was behind them—not that they would have acknowledged him if they had. They were talking about the delay at security.

"I overheard it was some Chinese lady," Erik was saying. "She had, like, a bomb or something, bro."

"No way, dude. They would have evacuated the entire airport for something like that," Derek said, his words lisped because of his invisible braces.

"Okay, maybe not a bomb. Maybe it was just some, like, ground-up shark fin or bat or something. But it was *definitely* a Chinese woman with something weird. You know how they are. I overheard some security dudes talking about it in the bathroom."

"My dad said they're, like, taking over the Philippines," Derek said.

"The security dudes?"

"No, idiot. The Chinese."

"Oh, yeah, bro. I heard that, too. When my tito visited over Christmas, he said the same thing."

As Erik and Derek continued dropping more shade about Chinese people, AJ tried to tune them out. Being one of a few brown kids in his school, he'd often heard his white classmates or teachers say similar things about different groups of people. But he expected better from kids whose families were immigrants or descendants of immigrants. Made no difference if their relatives had come over in the 1930s like AJ's, or if they'd come over recently, like Saul. They should know better.

A sick feeling settled into the pit of his stomach, and he was embarrassed to be wearing the same warm-ups as Erik and Derek. Everyone within earshot probably assumed he believed all these things, too.

Ugh, AJ messaged Saul. Now they're being super racist.

To you? Saul asked.

Nah. They're talking about Chinese people.

You should say something! #StopAAPIHate #AsianSolidarity

AJ considered this. What would he even say?

Maybe he could ask them how'd they feel if someone were spouting off stupid stereotypes about Filipinos. But what good would that do? At best, they'd ignore or laugh at him. At worst, they'd get into a fight that he'd definitely lose, and they'd all get in trouble with Coach.

#ImCool, he messaged Saul.

Saul didn't reply.

Thankfully, Erik and Derek fell quiet as they lost themselves in their phones. The line shuffled forward, the menu board now as close as the hoop from the top of the key.

But the peace didn't last.

Without looking up, Derek suddenly asked, "Dude, you think we got *any* shot of winning this thing without Saul?"

Erik shrugged. "I don't know, man. The two of us dominate down low, but we won't make it far if AJ can't step up."

"For real," Derek said. "Dude's decent in practice, but he's butt under pressure."

AJ's cheeks grew hot, but he couldn't be mad. It was true.

He loved shooting around in the driveway or playing pickup, but he hated the pressure of official games. The less time he spent on the court, the fewer failures his mind could collect. The only reason he was even on the team was because of Saul.

AJ had always been the only Filipino kid in his school until Saul showed up last year. At lunch on his first day, Saul had walked over to where AJ was reading a graphic novel alone at a table in the corner and asked, "Pilipino ka ba?"

AJ looked up from his book, face lit with a smile. It was the very first time at school that he'd ever heard the language that filled his home. "Oo," he said.

Saul fist-bumped AJ, then sat down, and they hit it off instantly. Turned out he had just moved to the US from Bicol in the Philippines, the same region AJ's family was from. They both played basketball, idolized Steph Curry, and loved the spaghetti with banana ketchup at Jollibee. They both disliked karaoke and bagoong and the Philippines' four-month-long Christmas season.

They hung out together after school that day, and the next, and every day after that. Mostly they played basketball or video games or read comics while AJ taught Saul how to survive in an American middle school and Saul helped AJ practice his Tagalog.

Then, a few months ago, Saul found out about the Filipino American youth basketball league in the city. Even though AJ had no desire to play anywhere other than in his driveway, Saul persuaded him to join a team with promises that the concession stands would sell lumpia, siopao, and bibingka in addition to hot dogs, nachos, and pizza.

"What do you think Saul's deal is, anyway?" Erik continued.

"What do you mean?" Derek said, still staring at his phone.

"Like, dude always shows up for every single practice. Never even a minute late. He's, like, the only one of us not running on Filipino Time. Coach included. But then he skipped all those practices, straight up missed our game last weekend, and then didn't tell anyone he was going to be MIA for this tournament. It doesn't make any sense."

AJ shifted.

Derek shrugged. "Maybe he thinks he's Iverson now or something."

"Nah, bro, he's good but not that good."

"Yo, I remember—my dad said he heard Saul's family is mad poor. Like, they live in a shack in the slums or something, back in the Philippines. You know, like those pictures you see online. They make a living by, like, scavenging garbage. He probably couldn't afford to come with us."

AJ's heart started pounding, and his palms got sweaty. Now he really wanted to say something, and he didn't want to vent to Saul, since he didn't want Saul to know they were trash-talking him. While it was true that Saul's family didn't have much money, they weren't living in the slums. And even if they were, what did that matter?

"For real?" Erik asked.

"For real."

"Hold up, bro," Erik said, brow furrowing. "If dude's family is mad broke, then how'd they even get to the States? They stow away on a ship or something?"

"Nah, they're still there. They just managed to scrape together enough to send him over here to live with his tita."

"So, dude's like an orphan?"

"Guess so."

AJ knew that's not what an orphan is, but he held his tongue again.

"Well, that explains a lot."

"Yeah, like his stench."

They both laughed.

"And how he wears the same shorts every practice."

Laughter.

"And his jacked-up teeth."

More laughter.

"And his messed-up sneakers."

They kept laughing.

"And how his cell phone's older than me."

They went on, cracking up as they tried one-upping each other roasting Saul. AJ wanted to defend his friend. To tell these fools the real reason Saul wasn't there—or at least say that Saul's family being poor wasn't something to laugh at. Tell them that all those things they were making fun of were the least important things about Saul.

Tell them instead to notice the way Saul slipped as easily between two languages and two cultures as he did through the lane. Or the way he was always willing to help someone out, just like he was always willing to make the extra pass. Or the way he made AJ feel not so alone anymore.

But the same thought that stopped him from speaking up when they were saying racist things about Chinese people stopped him from saying anything now: What was the point if it wouldn't change anything?

Instead, he stepped out of the line and walked away.

♀ ♀ ♀

AJ's brain didn't limit its lowlight reels to basketball. It would play any kind of mistake on repeat—bombing a test, dropping his phone and cracking the screen, forgetting to take out the garbage—until he felt like he was going to throw up.

So, as he strolled back toward their gate amid the river of travelers, hands buried in his pockets and backpack feeling twice as heavy as before, he kept thinking about how he'd stood there and said nothing, did nothing.

He'd simply opted out, walked away.

He tried to convince himself he'd staged some silent protest by leaving. He'd *chosen* to separate himself from his teammates to signal that he was not like them. Stepping out of line also meant he was sacrificing pizza—no small thing, especially given the time he'd already spent waiting.

So, from that perspective, hadn't walking away been kind of . . . *noble*?

Not full-on noble. Not like Gabriela Silang leading the Ilocano resistance against the Spanish. Or like José Rizal, whose writing and execution inspired Filipinos to continue fighting for independence. Or like Larry Itliong helping Filipino American farmworkers demand better conditions. Or like any of the other ancestors AJ's mom always taught him about—and whose stories make him glow with Pinoy pride—since she knew he wouldn't learn about them in school. Basically, not the full-on noble that resonated through history.

But a *kind-of* noble. Like giving-up-your-seat-on-the-bus-to-an-old-person noble. Or feeding-a-stray-cat noble. Or returning-someone-else's-shopping-cart-to-the-corral-because-they've-got-their-hands-full-with-kids noble. A quieter, kind-of noble.

If AJ's decision to walk away in silent protest were any type of noble, though, then why was it looping in his mind like a last-second air ball? Why did he feel his cheeks burning and the familiar shame of screwing up royally?

He shifted his heavy backpack, trying to find a more comfortable position. Maybe he should have explained the truth about why Saul wasn't coming—that he *couldn't* leave the country like everyone else, not even for a basketball tournament in Canada. After he didn't show up at the game last week, he had told AJ that he had overstayed his visa, so if he left the US now, they'd never let him back in. But Saul had also told AJ not to tell anyone that he was undocumented, so wasn't *not* saying anything the right thing to do?

AJ reached the crowded gate back in Concourse E where his coach and some of the other players waited, gathered in a circle on the floor. Swinging his backpack to the ground, he hung out at the edge of the group for a moment. But he didn't feel like being around them, so he picked the bag up again and wandered off, ending up on a moving walkway that carried him away from his teammates.

His phone buzzed with a text from Saul. So did you say something?

AJ put his phone back into his pocket without replying.

He let his eyes scan the people flowing past. Among the crowd of stressed-out travelers, there was a guy with a baby strapped to his chest and two twin toddlers frantically orbiting him as he hauled a backpack, pulled a roller bag, and pushed an empty double stroller. Dude looked like he could use an extra pair of hands or two.

Then there was an airport worker struggling to pull the bag out from one of the trash cans. It was caught on something, but she couldn't see that and kept tugging to the point where it was about to tear. And people kept reaching around her to toss in more garbage.

As the moving walkway carried him past the father and the airport worker, AJ felt bad for them. He felt bad for everyone who needed help that wasn't coming. Sometimes the world was unfair to people for no reason at all.

He reached the end of the moving walkway and was about to step onto the next one when he heard a girl's voice shout, "Hey!"

He stopped and turned around to look, along with a bunch of other people. It was a girl around his age. "Sorry," she said, now that people were paying attention, "but does anyone speak Tagalog?"

AJ's Tagalog wasn't great, so he hung back, waiting for someone else to step up. But the people who had gathered around looked confused. Most shook their heads and turned away. A few muttered, "What's Tagalog?" Some lingered just to watch.

There was a dude in a suit nearby who definitely looked Filipino, but he glanced at his watch, then dipped. Either he didn't speak the language or he couldn't be bothered to spare a few minutes.

It hit AJ that he was the only one who might be able to help.

He walked over to the girl, raising his hand like he was in school. "I speak Tagalog."

Relief washed over the girl's face. "Thanks," she said. She gestured to an old Filipina woman, who came forward, looking desperate and confused.

"I'm pretty sure she speaks Tagalog," the girl explained to AJ. "Her husband has a walker and is waiting down at their old gate—E37. Can you tell her this is her new gate?"

"Oh. Um, yeah. Yeah, I will."

AJ turned to the woman and translated as best as he could into Tagalog. It must have been good enough, because her face broke out in a smile as she thanked him.

The girl was also smiling, and AJ felt good about himself for the first time in a long time.

"I'll go ask someone to send a cart down to get her husband," he said, and then did.

The whole thing had only taken a couple of minutes, but now that woman and her husband would catch their flight because that girl had used her voice to speak up, and AJ had used his to help the woman.

AJ turned back the way he'd come and found the airport worker he'd seen struggling with the trash bag. It had apparently ripped open, spilling the garbage across the floor, and she was now gathering it all piece by piece. Instead of beating himself up for not helping her earlier, he went over and helped her pick everything up. She thanked him, and he noticed that her name tag read MYUNG.

Then AJ caught up with the father who had the baby and the toddlers and helped him move the roller bag and stroller to their gate.

The actions were small and didn't take much time. But they mattered. AJ could have passed these people without offering any help—he almost had because he'd been so caught up in thinking about all his failures. But that didn't stop him this time, and he resolved to not let it in the future.

As he walked back to his gate, his mind started replaying the ways he had helped in the last few minutes—a highlight reel, for once. He took out his phone and typed up a long text to Saul about all of it—but then he hesitated, thumb hovering over the Send button.

It wasn't about what someone else thought or did or saw. He did those things because they were the right thing to do, and he felt better for it. For once, he was proud of *himself*. That was enough. That was what mattered.

Even so, he tapped Send, because telling Saul about everything was as close as he was going to get to having his friend with him on this trip.

Right on! Saul replied, immediately followed by a string of brown raised-fist emojis.

#PinoyPower, AJ messaged.

Then Saul followed up with a GIF of Ari Agbayani, the Filipina Captain America.

AJ smiled. His good deeds were nowhere near super-hero-level, but maybe someday he could do more. Maybe all those noble Filipino heroes from history his mom taught him about didn't begin by leading revolutions. Maybe they started out by helping people in whatever small ways they could, in whatever small ways were needed. Maybe they built up to doing more, because maybe helping people was a skill that improved over time with practice, just like dribbling or passing or shooting a basketball.

AJ stopped in his tracks, travelers streaming past him as he thought. Walking past the girl or the airport worker or the father with the toddlers would have been like cutting practice—same as not saying anything to Erik and

Derek. That wasn't a kind-of-noble silent protest. AJ had simply made things easier for *himself* by staying silent, by walking away. He didn't have to feel the discomfort of listening to his teammates trash-talking and being racist. He didn't have to face the awkwardness of confronting them. He didn't have to deal with any consequences.

Nothing had changed except that *he* felt temporary relief.

What they had said wasn't right, and neither was AJ's silence. Just like that moment when AJ realized there was nobody else around who could—or would—translate Tagalog, he realized that nobody else was going to say anything to Erik and Derek if he didn't. AJ started forward again.

He didn't have to say anything about Saul being undocumented—that wasn't AJ's to share. Instead, he had to say something to get them to realize how mean and ignorant and hurtful they were being. Maybe it wouldn't change anything right away, but maybe it would get them to think twice about making fun of someone for not having enough money or for whatever reason. And he didn't have to deliver a speech or throw a punch. Maybe it was enough to call them out or ask the kind of question that would make them think.

Even if nothing actually came of it, AJ needed to do

what he felt was right.

When he reached the pizza place in the food court, Erik and Derek were stuffing pizza into their faces at a table meant for six, their bags and selves sprawled across the space.

AJ readjusted his backpack and cleared his throat. Determined to stand firm despite his heart thumping in his chest, he stepped up.

Natalie

Natalie Nakahara was a girl with a lot of feelings, which she collected the way some people collect teacups, or rocks, or Pokémon cards. There was, for example, that angry, splashy feeling she got whenever her little brother evicted one of her villagers in *Animal Crossing*; the fizzy, light-headed feeling she got whenever she and her best friend, Beth Martin, stayed up till 3 a.m. watching *Hunter x Hunter*; and the awed, quiet feeling she got whenever she glimpsed the vast gray of the Pacific Ocean at the end of her street. Sometimes, she even liked to try on a feeling to see how it fit, like once at her old school she'd tried being in love with Kenny Del Rosario from around the corner, but she didn't think the voluminous, swoopy feeling suited her—at least not yet—so after a week she got bored and stopped.

Ever since taking off from San Francisco with Beth

and her family, however, Natalie had been having a Weird Feeling, sort of flustery and twisted up, and this one wasn't mostly imaginary, like being in love with Kenny Del Rosario.

It all started when Mr. Martin, jittery on caffeine and excitement (a feeling Natalie recognized from every time she drank boba), turned around before takeoff and declared in a voice that practically rattled the overhead compartments, "And thus begins the Annual Martin Independence Day Cross-Country Extravaganza!" This was what the Martins called their yearly vacation in Vermont. "Are you ready, kids? Hot dogs, American flags, and fireworks! Everything you need for a good summer celebration!"

Beth rolled her eyes. "Ugh, Dad. Not everyone does fireworks, remember?"

Or eats hot dogs, Natalie thought as she fiddled with her seat belt. Actually, she'd never had hot dogs on Fourth of July. For her, the food that really made it feel like a holiday was Bachan's somen salad, which her family had been making for Independence Day since her great-great-grandparents had come to the United States over a century ago.

But she didn't want to seem impolite, especially since the Martins had paid for her plane ticket, so she didn't say anything.

Instead, she let the Weird Feeling fizzle away while she

and Beth dove into a deep discussion about the cosplay outfits they wanted to wear for their very first comic-con in August.

"Okay, so no one from *Ouran High School Host Club*, but what about *Demon Slayer*?" Beth asked, trading the bagel chips from her snack mix for Natalie's pretzels. (An unspoken I-know-this-is-your-favorite exchange.) "I still think you could go as Nezuko."

"I don't know . . . ," Natalie said, swirling the last of the ice in her cup. "What about the kimono?"

"What about it?"

"I've never worn one before." Actually, no one in her family ever dressed up like that, and the thought of asking Mom and Bachan to help her with the pink robe and checkered obi made her feel stiff and clompy. (A sneaking-into-your-mom's-closet-to-try-on-her-high-heels feeling.)

"What are you talking about? I think they'd be totally into it! You'd be *perfect* as Nezuko."

At her friend's unabashed encouragement, Natalie grinned, but she also couldn't help feeling a kernel of the Weird Feeling again. With thin brown hair and smooth, skim-milk skin, Beth was some mix of English and/or Irish and/or German and/or Dutch. She'd said she'd never really asked—and, Natalie had thought with a peppery dash of resentment, she'd never really had to think about it—so she didn't have any old traditions to feel weird about.

But it was such a small thing, really, and it wasn't like Natalie could explain all that anyway.

So she didn't.

Now she'd been standing in the food court at the Chicago airport for nearly fifteen minutes, waiting for Beth to pick up a pack of California rolls and watching nervously as Mr. and Mrs. Martin made nasty comments about some poor Asian kid who'd gotten his finger stuck in a chair while his sister was just trying to enjoy a Smashburger.

Enter: the Weird Feeling. Only this time it wasn't small, and it wasn't fizzling away.

(That buzzing in her head. That churning in her guts.)

With the rain streaming down the windows and the other passengers talking loudly on their cell phones, Natalie watched the girl speak up: "You're welcome!" Followed by the Martins' uncomfortable shifting. And the girl's triumphant walk. (A trumpet blast of a feeling.)

Then she locked eyes with Natalie and gave her a brilliant smile, and even though Natalie had stayed the night at the Martins' house and didn't even know the girl's name, it was like the two of them were a part of something. Something Mr. and Mrs. Martin, even though they were grown-ups, could never really understand.

And that was weird, wasn't it? To be so connected to

someone you'd never met and probably never would?

While she tried to puzzle it all out, she felt someone at a nearby table staring at her—a white man with straw-colored hair and windburned cheeks—his pale eyes boring into her like drill bits.

Natalie swallowed, wishing she hadn't worn her big red *Kiki's Delivery Service* hair bow, which made her stand out even in a large crowd like this one. (A fell-down-the-bleachers-during-a-school-assembly feeling.) Then again, to some people, maybe *any* Asian in a face mask was conspicuous—to them, maybe it didn't matter that Natalie was fifth-generation American and her family had been in this country since before World War I.

The man still hadn't stopped glaring at her, but before he could accuse her of carrying COVID or being one of the so-called Chinese smugglers from the TSA line, Beth squeezed into place beside her, shielding her from the man's view. "Are you ready?" she asked, more brightly than necessary.

Natalie nodded.

"Great! I just got a new cosplay idea. Let's find our seats so I can tell you all about it. . . ." Gently, Beth drew her away from the man's steely glare.

At the table, Mr. and Mrs. Martin were already half-way through their Starbucks, their trays dotted with empty sugar packets and stained coffee stirrers. While Natalie removed her mask, Beth clapped her hands together over her sushi and declared "Itadakimasu!" before cracking open the plastic shell.

"Itadakimasu," Natalie mumbled. Normally she liked repeating the phrase before digging into her meals, but right now the idea that Beth could go around speaking Japanese without a care in the world while Natalie couldn't even walk through the food court without drawing suspicion gave Natalie an uncomfortable, pebble-in-your-shoe feeling.

It wasn't Beth's fault, of course, but it was another of those small things, accumulating around Natalie little by little like dozens of tiny stones. Sighing, she opened a bag of Cheetos and used a pair of hashi from the sushi place to pop one of the puffs into her mouth.

"Hey, when did you start doing that?" Beth said, pointing.

"Doing what?"

"Did you learn it from your cousins or something?"

Natalie tried to swallow, but the Cheeto seemed to have turned to dust in her throat. She coughed. "You mean Mariko and Ryosuke?" she asked, stumbling embarrassingly over the *r*'s.

"So clever! No orange fingers!" Mrs. Martin chimed in with a smile. "I always say we could learn a lot from the Japanese about neatness, don't I?"

Natalie squirmed. *The Japanese?* She was Japanese American, which was different from being *from Japan*, and it's not like being from Japan automatically made you super tidy or anything—every time her cousins came to visit, they made a total mess of her room.

Besides, she'd learned the Cheetos-and-chopsticks trick from Kenny Del Rosario, who was Filipino American.

But she didn't want to make a bigger deal out of it than it already was, especially not in front of Beth's parents, who were watching her with toothy, expectant grins, so she just sat there awkwardly half smiling back at them. (A standing-in-a-rising-vat-of-Mountain-Dew feeling, fizzy and sticky on her skin.)

"Relax, you guys." Jonas, Beth's sixteen-year-old brother, sat down next to Mr. Martin with a boxed salad and a paperback he must have picked up from the terminal bookstore. "Just let her eat her lunch."

Beth and Mrs. Martin flushed an identical petal pink, and Natalie felt the sticky Mountain Dew feeling ebbing away. She liked Jonas, who had glints of gold in his eyes that reminded her of Edward and Alphonse from *Fullmetal*

Alchemist: Brotherhood, which was the only anime Jonas liked. Sometimes, even though she'd seen it, like, five times already, Natalie asked to rewatch it just so Jonas would sit on the couch with her and Beth, quietly smelling of half-hour shower and deodorant. (A pleasant, warm feeling, like sipping hot chocolate on a foggy day.)

"Okay," Beth said, dunking a California roll into a slurry of wasabi and soy sauce, "but I'm *so* doing that from now on!"

Natalie tried to smile. It came out twisted.

"Well, kids," Mr. Martin said, standing, "we're going to take the bags and get a seat near the gate before the boarding area gets even more full. Jonas, will you watch Natalie and your sister?"

"*Dad*," Beth protested. "We don't need to be *watched*."

Jonas didn't bother looking up from his paperback. "Yeah, whatever."

Natalie breathed a sigh of relief. (A sudden air-lock-pressure-release kind of feeling.) It's not that she disliked Mr. and Mrs. Martin, really, but as one small thing piled up on top of another, she couldn't help but feel the weight of Beth's parents near her, oppressive as a planet.

While Mr. and Mrs. Martin shuffled from the food court, carry-ons in tow, Beth turned to Natalie. "Okay, lemme tell you my idea. What do you think about me going as Mikasa?"

"Ooh!" Natalie brightened. (A sparkler of a feeling.) Mikasa Ackerman was a biracial Hizuruian-Eldian character from *Attack on Titan*, one of their favorite shows, and she was amazing. She was definitely the best fighter besides Captain Levi, and in the first three seasons she wore a uniform of slim khaki pants and a cropped jacket that would look so good on Beth. "You'd be great as Mikasa!"

Beth beamed. "You think so? I was thinking I could buy most of the pieces, but I could probably knit my own scarf, right? Then maybe I could dye my hair black, but I wasn't sure how to do the eyes."

The Weird Feeling hit Natalie like a whirlwind. (A torpedoed feeling, a sinking-ship feeling.) "The eyes?" she repeated, hoping she hadn't heard right.

"Yeah, the eyes." Briefly, Beth put her fingertips to her temples. She frowned thoughtfully. "I wonder what white actors do, you know, when they want to look Asian?"

Natalie didn't know why, but the thought of Beth Martin taping the corners of her eyes gave her a food-poisoning feeling, like when you didn't know *what* you ate, but your insides knew it was bad as soon as it hit your stomach, and they started to turn inside out just to get rid of it.

"I don't think that's a good idea," she said uneasily.

"Why not?" Beth crossed her arms, as if Natalie had insulted her. "If you were going to go as Jiji, you'd wear cat ears, wouldn't you? This is the same thing."

Natalie grimaced. That couldn't be right, could it? It *sounded* like it could be right, except it gave her the same upset-stomach feeling as before. But she *really* didn't want to fight in the middle of an airport while on vacation with her best friend's family, so she didn't say anything.

"Jesus, Beth." Jonas glared at his sister over the top of his book. "That's so racist."

"I'm not racist!" She stabbed at her sushi with her chopsticks. "Tell him, Natalie. I love everything about Japan."

Natalie stared uncomfortably at her Cheetos. She had too many feelings right now, and none of them were good. There was that flustery, twisted feeling she'd had all morning; plus a stinky-garbage-can feeling at how Beth was reacting; and a small, guilty feeling like maybe she shouldn't be so upset, because Beth was her friend, and it's not like she was being *mean* or anything, so what did Natalie have to be mad about?

But Beth's face was turning red now. Was she going to cry? Natalie *really* did not want her to cry—not in this public place, not when they'd have to spend three more

"A total monster!"

Beth laced her arm through Natalie's again, laying her head on her shoulder with a sigh. After a moment, her stomach rumbled, causing them both to giggle. "Ugh," she said. "I guess I should probably eat more than a couple stale California rolls. Want to go back?"

"Yeah." Behind her mask, Natalie grinned. "How about Smashburger?"

Standing, they left the bench and headed toward the food court, where Jonas straightened at the sight of them, waving them over.

"We're getting Smashburger!" Beth mouthed, pointing exaggeratedly at the busy restaurant.

Across the food court, Jonas took out his phone. Seconds later, Beth's text notification dinged: *Get me some fries.*

Shoving the phone back in her pocket, she rolled her eyes.

As they joined the burger line, they passed three boys in red-and-white warm-ups, two of them seated at a table strewn with pizza crusts and greasy napkins. Over the roar of the food court, Natalie overheard the smallest of the boys talking to his teammates: ". . . what you said about Chinese people . . ." and ". . . not cool . . ."

His next words were drowned out by the noise, but she did hear the taller boys' uncomfortable laughter, followed by "Nah, bro" and "Hold up, bro," and even though their protests were different from Beth's, Natalie instantly recognized their hurt, their resistance, their defensiveness.

The boy who had been speaking hesitated. (A precarious feeling, like trying to tightrope-walk between staying silent and letting things accumulate until they were too big to be ignored or forging onward through the awkwardness and pain of speaking up.) Then he smiled.

It came out twisted.

Natalie knew exactly how he felt. And, remembering the look she'd shared with the girl in the food court earlier, she knew how much that little moment of connection had meant to her. Catching the boy's eye, Natalie tugged down her mask to offer him her own painful smile. An I've-been-there-too smile. A you're-not-alone smile.

The corner of his mouth twitched. After a second, he turned back to his teammates.

Ruefully, she covered her face again.

"Hmm . . ." Beside her, Beth was studying the menu. "So do you think your mom will help you with your Nezuko cosplay?"

"I think so." Natalie nodded. She didn't know exactly how she'd bring it up, and she didn't know how it was going to go. Maybe Bachan would be there. Maybe they'd open up some of her old steamer trunks, pulling out the brightly patterned cloth, still smelling of mothballs. Maybe the kimono would be too big for her. Maybe her steps in her mom's geta would be unsteady. But she was hopeful (a warm, fluttering feeling), and she had plenty of time to learn. "I'm going to ask her when I get home."

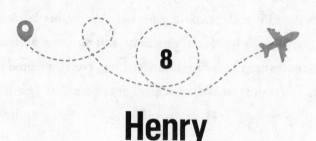

Henry

There were only two people from Henry Yun's family traveling to New Jersey that day, and it would have been unremarkable that Henry himself was the calmer of the two, if not for the fact that he was twelve years old, and the other person was his father. Henry hadn't always been the more calm one, but then again, Henry's parents hadn't always been divorced. "The only constant in life is change," Henry's mom liked to say. Henry knew that was true, but he also knew being true didn't stop it from being a giant pain in the butt.

The thing Henry had heard back in the security line didn't help, either. It'd been several minutes since Henry's ears had been assailed by the sound of someone talking in an insultingly fake Asian accent, real "ching chong" kind of stuff. And even though he and his dad had put their belts and shoes on the conveyor belt and were about to walk through the body scanner, he was still pretty agitated about it. To be fair, everyone in the airport was pretty agitated by then, since whatever had gone on in the security line had been bad enough to make TSA shut one line down entirely.

"You hanging in there, buddy?" asked James Yun, the less calm of the two Yuns (by just a little bit, to be fair), as they put their shoes back on and started toward their gate. James was an academic librarian who often went to conferences—he served on committees and the like—and so spent a lot of time in airports. The committee work sounded like the most boring thing on the planet to Henry, but he liked that his dad always brought home a bunch of free books that hadn't been officially published yet—*advanced promotional copies*, the publishers called them. Henry liked books more than almost anything, except maybe cats and donuts.

What Henry didn't like was his dad getting upset, so he was relieved to be the only one who'd noticed what had happened back at security—it would have set his dad off, for sure, and Henry wasn't about to tell him what he'd missed—but he also felt a little ashamed about not having done anything, because wasn't racism something people should stop? But what if "people" meant *him*, Henry, who'd never met a fight he wasn't willing to run away from? His aikido sensei always talked about walking away from fights unless they were unavoidable. That made sense to Henry, but he'd actually started taking aikido classes to learn *how* to fight, because bullies were everywhere, and he was tired of being afraid of them, and anyway, he wasn't even sure there was a connection between keeping secrets from his dad and walking away from a fight in the first place.

Ugh. Life is complicated.

"I'm okay, Dad—I bet this trip's less stressful than when I was four and we flew to Washington, DC, right?" Henry said. It was a blatant attempt to change the subject, but Henry knew it would probably work, because that kind of thing usually worked on Henry when other people did it to him.

"You remember that, do you?" James knew full well that Henry didn't remember, but Henry understood the question was part of his dad's routine when telling the story, and he didn't mind. It was an entertaining story, after all.

"No, Dad. I was *four*."

"Right, too young to remember—you had a meltdown every time we had to leave one part of the airport and go to another one," James said, looking around and sweeping his hand up in an arc as they passed a crowded gate and entered an empty stretch of the concourse with no seats at all.

"Totally kicking and screaming, right?" Henry said. James laughed, and Henry relaxed a little. Taking care of his dad was a lot of work.

"Kicking and screaming while *lying on your back*, even," James said.

Henry snorted in amusement.

"Scarred for life," James said. "Your mom and I, that is."

Henry very obviously and visibly rolled his eyes, even though the joke was honestly really good for a dad joke.

"Hey, don't roll your eyes at me," James said, making an equally exaggerated scowl.

Henry stared at his dad with an extremely fixed, bug-eyed expression. He started to veer into the flow of foot traffic coming the other way, and James gently course-corrected Henry with a hand on his shoulder.

"This is when your mom would tell us we're both acting like cartoon characters," James said. "Have I told you about the time my friend Brian's mother said that to me?"

"Yep," Henry said. "*Were* you acting like a cartoon character?"

"I'm sure I was trying to act friendly and whatnot, like a neurotypical person. I was teaching myself how to do it, but I wasn't very good at it yet. I'm glad you've had better help with that."

They both lapsed into silence and stayed that way as they walked through the airport, noting the locations of the bathrooms, the food court, and—Henry was excited to see—a bookstore. Both of them would feel better once they'd actually found the gate they'd be leaving from, but Henry would be sure to come back to the bookstore once they'd done so. As they walked past, Henry heard someone inside talking like they were on a phone.

"Yeah, the flight's been delayed indefinitely. . . . I know, right? Who brings that kind of stuff through security? Foreigners . . ."

And just like that, Henry's excitement fizzled out.

"Dad."

"Yes, big boy?"

"Do you ever get scared?"

James looked sideways at Henry, who was looking at his own hands and noticing the contrast in texture between his wrinkly palms and the smooth fuzziness of the carpet as his feet moved across it.

"Now, that is an interesting question," James said. "Scared of what, exactly?"

Henry shrugged. "I don't know. People, I guess."

James thought about it for a minute, fiddling with the black wire of his glasses frame. "Yes," he said, at last. "Not always for the same reasons, but sometimes, yes."

Henry nodded. "Me too."

"Henry, did something happen that I missed?"

Yes, but I'm not telling you what it was, and ugh.

"No," Henry said, wincing internally. "I mean, not just now, but . . ."

James wasn't a perfect parent, and he and Henry both knew it, but one thing he did know how to do was wait patiently while Henry figured out what to say—and whether he actually wanted to say it. They walked on, catching the occasional glimpse of a plane or a baggage truck outside the terminal windows.

"There's a lot of mean people," Henry said finally, unable to articulate something better.

"In the world, you mean," James said.

"In the world, at school, probably in this airport . . ."

"I'm sorry," James said unhelpfully. "Best to let it go."

· Henry gave his dad a stink eye look that he sometimes used for comic effect, although not this time. "I hate feeling scared, Dad."

"I do, too, big boy. It's not a good feeling."

Henry sighed. "People are the worst," he said.

"Sometimes."

"And people are confusing."

"*All* the time, yes," James said with a very restrained smile.

"I know it's an autistic thing, but some autistic things suck," Henry said, suddenly feeling tired.

"I'm sorry, kiddo."

They reached their gate, found an empty row of seats, and sat down, carefully arranging their bags on the seats on either side of them, like a layer of insulation against other travelers. The big digital sign at the check-in desk was showing their flight information, but the only word that really mattered right then was "delayed." James went over to talk with the gate agent and came back shaking his head.

"Sorry, buddy, they don't actually know when our flight will take off—the airport's a total mess right now."

"Yay for us," Henry said.

They sat for a few minutes, recovering from the noisy walk across the airport and thinking, and Henry leaned sideways and rested his head against his dad's arm, glad that at least they were together.

"Is Halmoni going to be weird about the autistic thing?" Henry asked, voicing his biggest worry about their trip.

"About you being autistic? Or about me being autistic?"

"About *anyone* being autistic, Dad. But yeah, especially me, now that I've been diagnosed. And I guess you, too, since you've been diagnosed as well."

James smiled. "I *am* her son, and that part's relevant. Weird in what way?"

"I don't know, in, like, telling me not to stim because it'll bring bad luck, or talking about all her friends and their kids, none of whom I've ever met, or whatever. When she does that, I feel like I'm gonna fall into a coma."

James shrugged. "She probably will talk about them, but that's not just your halmoni, buddy. That's every grandparent, parent, aunt, and uncle on the planet. *Everyone's* older relatives talk about their friends, and their friends' kids, and other people you don't know or care about, whether anyone in the room's autistic or not."

"Great."

"Also, I don't think your halmoni will be weird because *you're* autistic and everyone knows it now," he said. "I think it's because *she's* autistic but doesn't know it, and wouldn't ever talk about it if she did."

Henry took a moment to let that wind through his brain as he stared at the concourse, where an uneven stream of people kept rushing by, much like the thoughts in his head. A girl marched past, looking very purposeful, followed by a younger boy with a unicorn sticker on his face.

"Come on, Ezzie," the girl called back to the boy, who hurried to catch up and let the girl take his hand. They vanished around a corner. *Cool sticker*, Henry absently thought before turning back to his father.

"What do you think would happen if I asked Halmoni if she's autistic, too?" he said.

James snorted. "Oh, she'd say no—like I said, she has no idea. You gotta remember your halmoni's Korean, like, *Korean* Korean, not Korean American. A lot of Koreans from her generation aren't super enlightened about neurodivergence. Or therapy. Or anything about mental health."

"Ugh," Henry said. "So, I'm too autistic *and* I'm not Korean enough, because I'm autistic and talk about it?"

James snorted again. "Knock it off with the 'too autistic' and 'not Korean enough.' You're the perfect amount of both."

Henry considered that for a moment. "Is there an imperfect amount of either?"

"No."

Henry nodded. "Okay. Can we stop talking about this and go to the bookstore already?"

"Of course! We can't be in an airport and *not* go to the airport bookstore. What kind of father do you think I am?"

Henry cupped his chin in his fingers, being certain to

really exaggerate it, so his dad would know he was kidding. "Hmm . . . an autistic dad, a Korean dad—"

"Korean *American*," James said. "Just plain Korean is different, you know."

"Yeah, yeah," Henry said, gathering his bags. "Okay, a Korean American dad, a librarian dad, a dad who yells at everyone, then apologizes to everyone over and over and over and over—"

"Aw, now you're just being mean," James said, using an exaggerated sad voice, so Henry would know *he* was kidding.

"Well, you raised me," Henry said, leading his father to the bookstore.

Henry and James, who were both very methodical about shopping for books, got down to business when they entered the store. First, they looked at the books, *all* the books, then the magazines, then back to the books, where they made their top five picks, which they narrowed down to three, then two, then one. Henry disliked how small the selection of books was—especially the kids' books—in comparison to non-airport bookstores, but it was a lot better than having no bookstore at all.

"There are never any books about autistic Korean characters," Henry said as they waited in line. He grabbed a chocolate bar from the display in front of the cash registers. "Can I get one of these?"

"My Father of the Year campaign will take a hit if I let you eat that, but since we're on vacation, I'll make an exception," James said. "And you can't expect too much from an airport bookstore, especially since there are never any books about autistic Korean characters, even in the really good bookstores."

"Somebody needs to write those," Henry said.

"Maybe that'll be you, Henry."

"Hmm. Maybe." After taking a few minutes to process the idea, Henry asked, "Do you really think I could, Dad?"

"Do what?" James said, looking up from the copy of *Crying in H Mart* he'd decided to buy, despite already having a copy at home. (Henry did a survey of all of his dad's books every year or so, just to know what his future reading options were.)

"Write a book about an autistic Korean American character."

"Yes," James said as he gently closed his book, "I do. I think that with time and practice, you could do that very well."

They left the bookstore feeling recharged, partly because of the new books, partly because the store had been relatively empty—which was always less stressful for both father and son—and partly because Henry was *very* absorbed by the idea of writing a book starring an autistic Korean American character, a book in which someone like him got to be the hero.

I could write a story about an aikido student, he thought. *An autistic, Korean American aikido student who likes cats and donuts. Or maybe who has a cat* named *Donut.*

The prospect of food brightened their moods further, and after successfully acquiring a sausage-and-mushroom pizza, they felt downright cheerful.

"Hey, look, other Asian people," Henry said as they miraculously scored an empty booth at the end of the food court near a coffee stand. He pointed at two girls, one bigger than the other, standing in line at McDonald's. "Safety in numbers, right, Dad?"

"Not necessarily," James said.

"Geez, Dad, you're such an Eeyore." Henry slid into his seat in the booth.

"An Eeyore?" James said, rubbing his head with both hands, making his already messy hair stand up in spiky clumps. "I don't think so! And why is a crabby donkey from a book written by a British white man the first thing you can think of to call me?"

"It's not the first thing, it's just the most accurate thing," Henry said with a toothy grin. "Even British white men get it right sometimes—at least until I write my own book and come up with something better to call you."

James laughed. "You know who's not Korean enough?" he said.

"You," Henry said.

"That's right, me, because no self-respecting Korean dad would accept this kind of insolence from his son!"

"Yes, they would. Korean American dads aren't a monolith, you know."

"I *am* a Korean American dad," James said.

"And look at you being all not a monolith and everything!"

This time they both laughed.

"You're a great kid, Henry. I'm lucky to be your father."

"Thanks, Dad."

They stopped talking to tend to the serious business of finishing the pizza.

As James chewed his final bite, Henry carefully scraped up the last glob of cheese and toppings in the middle of the empty box, thinking about what kind of pizza his aikido-practicing character would prefer, and whether Donut the cat would try to eat any of the pizza or not.

"Hey, I need to use the bathroom," James said, tossing their used napkins into the pizza box and closing it.

"Can I meet you at the gate?" Henry said, thinking it

might be nice to have a few minutes to himself.

"Sure, I'll be right there."

As Henry started back toward the gate, imagining reasons why his character might be at an airport, two boys—one who looked about Henry's age, and one who was definitely younger—came out of an electronics store up ahead, saw Henry, and started snickering as they approached.

Henry felt his body stiffen up, and suddenly it felt awkward just to be walking. At the same time, his mind went into overdrive. Henry's brain was always full of thoughts, not just one thought, and not just some thoughts, but all the thoughts at once, all the time. So, in that moment, he saw in his mind all the bullies who'd ever come at him, and he felt every molecule of humiliation he associated with always backing away from them. And then a new thought entered his mind: *My autistic aikido character wouldn't back away.*

The taller boy said something behind his hand to the shorter boy, and as they passed by, he veered to the side and walked right at Henry, who knew from experience that the boy's intent was to drive his shoulder right into Henry's and knock him off-balance.

Henry saw it coming, and a cluster of thoughts popped into his head—not chaotically, as they so often did, but softly, calmly, and powerfully. He thought about his sensei teaching an exercise about not letting people get in your way:

"When your partner tries to stop you from walking, keep your shoulders down, keep moving your arms like in a rowing exercise, and stay grounded. Feel your connection to the earth, and simply keep walking. If you have to, you can walk right through your partner."

He thought about writing a story where an autistic Korean American kid was the hero.

He thought about being the hero of his *own* story.

And then Henry acted.

He didn't wait for the other boy to hit him first. He dropped his shoulders, and right before the moment of contact, he subtly pivoted on his back foot so his body was almost pointing at the other boy. The boy's shoulder hit the side of Henry's shoulder, with Henry's entire body aligned behind it, and the very satisfying result (at least for Henry) was that the boy more or less bounced off Henry, lost his balance, and staggered diagonally backward, pinwheeling his arms, for a good ten feet, until he collided with an airline pilot who was pulling a rolling suitcase behind him. The other boy laughed loudly, braying, "That was hysterical!"

"Shut up, Jake!" the taller boy said, saved from hitting the floor only by the pilot's quick catch. "I'm warning you!"

"What are you going to do, Oliver? Fall down on me?" Jake nearly collapsed in a fit of laughter as both boys turned to leave.

The pilot shook his head, stood his fallen suitcase back up, tipped his hat to Henry, and walked off, just as Henry's dad arrived at a run.

"Henry!" James said, trying to look in three directions at once. "What the heck just happened?"

"Mean people," Henry said serenely. "They left, though."

"Yeah, I saw that part, at least—are you okay?" James said, running both hands furiously through his hair (which he must have combed in the bathroom) until his head once again resembled a black-and-gray porcupine.

"Totally okay." Henry looked at his dad, feeling good in the strangest way. He felt calm. He felt grounded. He felt *right*. He was also very glad to see his dad, even though he was a little impatient with him for being so agitated.

Father and son looked each other in the eye for quite a bit longer than either of them could usually handle, until James finally twisted up one corner of his mouth in what Henry liked to call a pseudo smile, which was when Henry tackle-hugged him.

"Oof," James said as they wrapped their arms around each other. "I guess you really are okay." He sounded confused, but it didn't stop him from giving Henry his customary kiss on the head.

"Can we move out of the way of all these people?" Henry said.

"Of course," James said. "Tell you what, let's go back to the food court and sit down—we can check our flight's status first."

Their flight was still delayed indefinitely, so they back-tracked to the food court and miraculously arrived just as a young-looking couple got up from a two-person table at the very edge of the food court, where it was least crowded. Henry sat, and James plunged into the increasingly hectic maw of the food court. He returned with coffee for himself and a bottle of juice for Henry, who reached across the table and took his dad's hand.

"Are you going to tell me what happened with those boys?" James asked.

The word "no" automatically came almost all the way to Henry's lips, but he caught it before saying it out loud, and thought hard about what to actually say.

Dad will freak out! I need to take care of him. I'm sick of keeping secrets from Dad. It feels horrible! But if I don't take care of him, who will? It's hard enough just trying to take care of myself! Wait, I did just take care of myself.

Maybe Dad can take care of himself, too.

Henry took a breath. "The taller kid tried to start something with me, and I didn't let him," he said.

James looked at him with a wide-eyed, skeptical expression on his face.

"You know that book about an autistic Korean American aikido student I'm going to write? The character with a cat named Donut?"

James's face went blank, which was a relief, because Henry knew it wasn't due to a lack of emotion or belief; it was the opposite, in fact. Right then, no expression on his dad's face meant no *disbelief*. It meant he was listening.

"The book, yes, all of those details, no," James said, and Henry loved him for responding so seriously, and so precisely.

"Well, I was thinking about my character, and how he wouldn't back away from bullies, and when that boy came at me and tried to make me move, I didn't. Then the other kid laughed at him, and then they left."

"And that was it?"

Henry nodded.

"And you're okay?"

"Yes."

James was silent for a moment. Then, surprisingly calm, he said, "Okay. Well, I'm impressed."

It was Henry's turn to look at his dad, his eyes so wide

open, it felt like his forehead was rolled all the way back over the top of his head. James snorted.

"Is that so much of a surprise?" he said.

Henry shrugged. "Not really, but it's kinda nice to hear it."

"Hmm," James said. "That probably means I should say it more often, since I'm always impressed with you."

"Well, if it makes you feel better, I'm even more impressed with myself," Henry said.

James grinned. "Do you remember the time we flew to Washington, DC, when you were four?"

"Dad. We already talked about that, like, an hour ago."

"Oh, right," James said. "Sorry."

"It's fine, Dad."

"It's just that . . . I'm just realizing how long it's been since that trip. You're not four years old anymore."

"Nope," Henry said.

"That's right. You're growing up, big boy. I'm not gonna lie: it's a little strange."

"You're a little strange, too, Dad, but I still love you."

"I love you, too, Henry, and I'm proud of you. Really, really proud."

"Thanks, Dad."

James drained the remainder of his coffee. "So, this book character is based on yourself, right?" he said.

Henry blinked. "Umm . . . no? That's not how I was thinking about it."

"That's what it sounds like to me, big boy. Guess you did some real character-development work while I was in the bathroom, huh?" James reached over to stroke Henry's hair.

"I guess so." Henry smiled.

"Hey, can you wait here for a minute?" James said. "There's something I want to get. Be right back!"

Henry watched his father jog down the concourse, dodging around the occasional slow-walking group of travelers, and vanish into a store. A few minutes later James reemerged and hurried toward Henry with a bag in his hand.

"Wow, that was fast," Henry said as his father sat down.

"There were a lot of people in there, too," James said in between huffs and puffs. "Nobody was in line, though, and I already knew what I wanted to buy."

He reached into the bag and pulled out a notebook. Not just a plain old composition notebook like the ones Henry used for school, but a superfancy one. It was hardcover, bound in very soft green leather, and just the right size to fit into Henry's mini backpack without risking damage to the corners. James put it into his son's hands. Henry opened to a blank page, and the paper was heavy, firm, and the color of a solidly white eggshell—which was a very good color for writing on, in Henry's opinion. "I remembered seeing it earlier," James said, "and I thought it might be useful for that book you're going to write."

"This is awesome, Dad. Thanks!" Henry felt a wave of gratitude and affection for his dad, which was extra nice to feel while they were in a loud, crowded, potentially hostile airport.

"Henry," James said.

"Dad," Henry said.

"Question."

"Yes. Also, this conversation is happening one word at a time."

James laughed. "Well, not anymore. So, when you write this book . . . could I read it? And it's okay to say no."

"Do you think you can handle it?" Henry said, partly joking and partly serious.

"Yes," James said decisively. "Do *you* think I can handle it?"

A few moments of comfortable, patient silence went by as Henry considered this question, which had no precedent in the twelve-year epic tale of James and Henry Yun, Father and Son.

"Yes," he said, finally, quietly.

"Wonderful," James said. "Thank you."

"You're welcome. Is it okay if I start working on it now?" Henry said, unzipping his backpack and pulling out a pen and his noise-blocking headphones.

James smiled and nodded. "I can't think of a better way to use all this extra time in the airport."

Henry nodded, then slowly leaned over the table with his head at an angle. James did the same thing, and when their heads made contact, they held them there long enough for James to whisper "I love you," and for Henry to whisper "Dada" before sitting up straight again. Henry put on his headphones and opened the notebook to the first page, taking a moment to run his fingertips slowly and lovingly across the heavy paper. Then he picked up his pen, took a deep breath, bent over the notebook, and started to write.

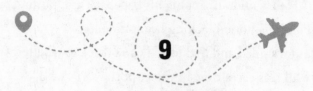

9

Camilla

I don't know if you have a special spot on the couch, but I do. The corner of the sectional next to the end table, where my Gatorade is in perfect reaching distance. There's a blue pen mark on the cushion. No one knows it's there but me, because I'm the one who accidentally swiped the couch when I was doing my homework two years ago. That's why I started sitting there in the first place, to hide the pen mark from my mom. But it's become my special spot. And that's where I want to be right now, watching stand-up comedy specials on Netflix with my dad, laughing until we snort.

My dad and I have the same laugh.

My mom and I don't have the same anything.

So, instead of being in my special spot with my legs propped up and snort-laughing as I open a fresh bag of Tostitos, I am sitting next to my mother in the food court of the Chicago airport. We are on our way to the Philippines. We haven't even left the United States, and I already want to go home. And there is nothing fun about that.

It wasn't fun when my mom, my eight-year-old sister, Greta, and I had to lug fifty-pound suitcases to the ticket counter at the Houston airport this morning to fly here. It wasn't fun when I had to sit on a cramped plane listening to Greta's cartoons blaring through her earbuds. And it wasn't fun when we had to wait a million years to deplane because people took forever to gather their bags, only to find ourselves at *another* airport with a fifty-year layover for our next flight, which will take us to New York, then to Manila, where we'll have to get on a bus to find our mother's hometown, which is so small it doesn't even appear in a Google search. Which means we've only just begun.

Okay, so the layover isn't really fifty years long. But it might as well be.

At least we don't have the big suitcases anymore.

Even Greta, who barely weighs fifty pounds herself, was forced to pull one behind her.

"This is so *heavy*," she said after our dad dropped us off for our first flight.

"You only have to bring it to the check-in counter," my mom said, her tiny hand wrapped around her own fifty-pounder. She called them our Big Day suitcases because when we arrived in the Philippines with them, it would be a "big day" for everyone. "And then we say goodbye to them."

"Good riddance," I mumbled.

The Big Day suitcases had dominated our lives for two weeks. My mother bought them secondhand, then announced that we needed to fill all three of them with stuff we didn't need or want anymore, as long as the items were in good condition. But the suitcases couldn't weigh more than fifty pounds apiece, or we'd have to pay extra money to put them on the airplane.

The plan was for us to bring them to my mother's hometown, where she would give everything away.

"What am I supposed to put in it?" I asked when she first brought the Big Day suitcase to my room and unzipped it. I stared at the gaping hole.

"Clothes, toys, books," she said, waving her hand toward my cluttered floor and shelves. "Anything you don't want."

"I want everything I have," I said.

This was only half-true. To be honest, I just didn't feel like packing the suitcase. But one thing I already knew for certain: my Texas A&M T-shirt would not go in any Big Day suitcase. My dad had given it to me for Christmas, because Texas A&M is his alma mater, and right then and there, as I contemplated the suitcases, I vowed to wear the shirt during the entire journey to the Philippines. If I had to travel across the world against my will, I wanted everyone to know where I came from.

"Ay, Camilla," my mom said. She swept her dark eyes over all my stuff—neglected dolls, old stuffed animals, piles of unworn clothes. "Think of Miralinda."

Ugh.

Miralinda. Miralinda. Miralinda.

I sighed. Loudly.

It always came back to Miralinda.

◉ ◉ ◉

Miralinda is my cousin. She is twelve, like me. She lives in the Philippines. We've never met, but I've heard her name my whole life. I know what she looks like, too, because my mom has forced me to scroll through pictures as she tells me about every relative who has ever lived. "This is your uncle Jun-Jun; it takes him three hours just to get to work one way," and "This is Tita Theresa; she is the best cook in the family."

And then—Miralinda.

My mom is convinced that Miralinda and I could be best friends. We were born only three days apart, my mom is all too happy to remind me, which means we're "practically twins." Miralinda's life is much different from mine.

For one thing, she has to walk through the mud to get to school, and she has only one pair of shoes. My mom reminds me of this any time I complain about the bus.

Mom also reminds me of how much Miralinda and I have in common.

"Miralinda loves garlic rice and tuna fish, just like you."

"Miralinda has a smile just like yours."

"Miralinda loves to dance in her room, too."

"Wait till you meet Miralinda! You'll have so much to talk about. Like best friends."

But I don't want to be best friends with a girl I've never met. I just want to be home, in our little house in Texas, with my dad. He couldn't take the time off work, so he stayed behind.

"Why can't I just stay with Dad?" I asked my mom, weeks ago, as we made pancit bihon. Pancit bihon is one of my favorite dishes. It's made with thin, translucent noodles and any kind of meat you want. I like chicken, and Greta likes pork, so my mom usually uses both. It's my job to chop the cabbage.

Mom always sings while she cooks. Cheesy love songs, usually. Filipinos love cheesy love songs, she says. She's not the best singer in the world, but don't tell her that.

"It's important to understand where you come from," Mom said. She stopped her rendition of Celine Dion's

"My Heart Will Go On" to click her tongue at my cutting board. "Make sure you chop them real good, Cam-Cam."

She calls me Cam-Cam sometimes. I don't mind. Her name is Lourdes, but people call her Lo. In addition to cheesy love songs, Filipinos love nicknames.

"But I don't come from the Philippines," I said. "I'm from here."

"Texas is part of you," she said. "But the Philippines is, too."

But she's the one from the Philippines, not me. I don't even *look* Filipino. I look just like my dad—light skin, light eyes, light hair, pointy nose. Greta got most of the Filipino genes.

"I don't *feel* Filipino, though," I said.

My mom paused. "What does Filipino feel like?"

I shrugged. "I don't know."

"I guess it's a good thing you're going to the Philippines, then," she said. Then she kept singing.

❈ ❈ ❈

I have never seen Greta wear a baseball cap before, but she's wearing one now. It's pulled low, shading the top of her face, and she's wearing a mask, so you can't see the bottom of her face, either. Her long, dark hair hangs down her back, but otherwise, Greta is hidden from the world, sitting across from me at the food court.

I lean forward. "Are you undercover?"

She lifts her head from her iPad. "What?"

I wave toward her face. "You look like you're under-cover. Your whole face is hidden. Are you trying not to be recognized? Are you hiding from—" I lean forward more and whisper, "the paparazzi?"

Greta shrugs. "I wear hats now. It's my thing."

"Since when?"

"Since forever."

"I've never seen you wear one."

"I wear them all the time, just like you always wear that dirty Texas A&M shirt," Greta says. "You just don't pay attention."

For the record, my shirt is *not* dirty. I wash it. Some-times. And this thing about Greta and baseball caps isn't true. Since Greta was born, I've spent every day of my wak-ing life with her, for better or worse, and she has never—not once—worn a baseball cap.

"Mom," I say, "have you ever seen Greta wear a base-ball cap before?"

Mom is scrolling through her phone. Facebook, prob-ably.

She glances up at Greta. "No, but it's a good look." She tilts her head. "You look tough. Like the Wolfman."

She means Wolverine.

The thought of Greta being anything like Wolverine makes me want to laugh, but I don't. Wolverine gets angry and breaks stuff. Greta barely speaks above a whisper when she's around people she doesn't know.

Greta lays her iPad carefully on the table. She's very delicate with all her things. Her Big Day suitcase is filled with immaculately clean dolls and books.

"Can I get something from Jamba?" Greta asks.

"Sure," Mom says. She reaches for her purse and pushes her chair back.

"I want *Camilla* to take me," Greta says. "Just me and Camilla."

Mom and I exchange looks.

"I'll take her," I say. "The line's not too long."

Mom gives me a twenty. As we walk away, she repositions her chair so she has a clear view of the Jamba line. My mom is convinced that me and/or Greta could be snatched up at any moment by a psychopath.

"Since when do you like Jamba?" I ask. "I've never even had it."

"Since Nora's mom took me," Greta says. Nora is her best friend. "I get an Aloha Pineapple smoothie. That's my drink. Nora gets blackberry. Gross." She pulls down her mask for a flash so she can stick out her tongue, just in case I wasn't sure how she felt about blackberry.

I study the menu as we get in line. I have no idea what to order. To be honest, I thought Jamba just had juice, but they have food, too. Now I don't know what I want—a smoothie or a sandwich? The smoothies look good, but so do the sandwiches. I try to listen to what people are ordering. Maybe it'll give me some inspiration. The girl in front of us looks like she already knows what she wants. She's not even paying attention to the menu. Maybe I should ask her for suggestions. She looks friendly enough. Maybe.

Greta is so excited about her Aloha Pineapple smoothie, she's bouncing on the balls of her feet. I once read that most dogs are food-motivated. Well, so are most Gretas, according to my research.

The line moves forward. The Maybe-Friendly Girl in front of me looks directly at the cashier—whose name is Riley, according to their name tag—and orders a Strawberries Gone Bananas smoothie and an oatmeal bowl with extra honey and extra brown sugar crumbles.

Now it's my turn. I decide I want a pumpkin smoothie, even though Elizabeth Finn, a girl in my class, says pumpkin is "so basic." I'm not one hundred percent sure why pumpkin smoothies are basic, but I like pumpkin, and Elizabeth Finn isn't here to judge, so I'm gonna order whatever I want.

I give Riley our order and step to the side. I'm shoving

change in my pocket when I hear it—a voice that suddenly sounds louder than everything else. It says, "Hopefully they go back to their own country and stay there."

As soon as I hear that, I get a really bad feeling in the pit of my stomach. That feeling when you know something terrible has happened—or *will* happen—and your heart plummets to your stomach and waits for life to get normal again.

My head snaps up, looking for whoever said it, and Greta steps behind me, like she's afraid the woman is talking to her. But from what I can tell, the woman—she has blond hair and a very pink sweater—is talking to these two white men near us. At first, I think the three of them are together, but one of the men pulls out his cell phone to record the conversation. From the look on his face, I can tell that he's not this woman's friend. The other man explains that Maybe-Friendly Girl is their daughter.

I'm not a genius or anything, but it doesn't take much to figure out what's going on. Maybe-Friendly Girl is Asian American, and this white woman said something about people going back to their own country.

The air suddenly feels heavy.

The woman has a kid with her. A boy. She pulls him away, muttering that she doesn't "have time for this." As the boy walks off, he tugs at the corners of his eyes and says,

"Kung Flu." All the muscles in my body stiffen. I glance at Maybe-Friendly Girl, to see her expression, to see if she's okay, and maybe—I don't know—to say something. But I don't know what to say. And I don't know how I would say it, because the oxygen has left the air around me. That's how it feels, anyway.

I can see our mom from here. Her chair is still pointed directly at the line. Her mask covers her nose and mouth, making her eyes the centerpiece of her face. She's too far away to hear the conversation, but she sees me and waves, as if to say, *Don't worry, I'm still here, just in case.*

I see someone else, too—a boy sitting across from a man with black glasses, eating pizza. They're also Asian. They're out of earshot, but it doesn't matter. It feels like I'm hearing everything for them, and something twists inside me.

I motion toward a two-person table nearby. My heart is still in my stomach. "Let's sit here while we wait."

Greta and I sit down, but neither of us says anything. I think about that woman. I don't see where she went. She's gone, but her words hover everywhere. And I think about that kid. *Kung Flu.* And I think about Maybe-Friendly Girl, who is still standing there.

"Was he talking to me?" Greta asks. She's slumped in

her chair, with her chin practically resting on her chest.

"Who?"

"You know," she replies. "That boy who said . . ."

Kung Flu.

"No," I say. "He was talking to the girl in front of us."

"Good."

"Good?"

"Well, not good for her, but good for me," Greta says. She looks up. The dark blue baseball cap still shades most of her face. "It means my disguise is working."

The bad feeling rises up again.

"Disguise?" I ask.

She pulls the cap lower. "So people don't see my face."

"Why don't you want people to see your face?"

"Because they say things like that boy," she says.

"Who is 'they'?"

She shrugs with one shoulder. "The kids at school. Like, Owen Montgomery and them. Owen's grandma got COVID, and he said it was my fault. And when they play Chinese Tag at school, I'm always It."

"Chinese Tag?"

I know I just keep repeating everything Greta is saying, but that's because she's never mentioned any of this before.

"Chinese Tag," Greta says matter-of-factly. "One person

is It, and you have to tag people to give them coronavirus. And I always have to be It." She sighs. "I wish our mom was like Nora's mom."

She means white.

Nora's mom and ours are different in many ways. Nora's mother drives an oversized Lincoln Navigator. Our mom drives a Toyota Prius. Nora's mother wears lipstick all the time, no matter what. Our mom can't be bothered. Nora's mother dances in the car at red lights. Our mom listens to power ballads.

But even knowing all that, I understand right away what Greta means.

If our mother were white, Greta wouldn't have to be It when they play Chinese Tag.

Riley the Cashier calls out to us. Our order is ready. Maybe-Friendly Girl is gone. So are the men with her, her dads.

I don't stand up right away, but Greta does. As we walk toward our smoothies, she says, "I don't want to be It anymore."

◗ ◗ ◗

When I was in fifth grade, I invited Elizabeth Finn for a sleepover. We watched movies and YouTube videos. We tried to see who could sing in the highest key, just for fun. We mismatched the wildest outfits we could find. We put sleeping bags in the family room and surrounded them with junk food. We stayed up past midnight—which was our goal—and finally lay down to sleep when it was almost one o'clock.

The house was quiet as we tried to drift off, until Elizabeth broke the silence.

"Why is your mom Chinese?"

I blinked into the darkness. "What do you mean?"

"Your mom is, like, Chinese or something, right? But you're not," she said.

"My mom isn't Chinese."

"She isn't?"

"No. She's Filipino."

"Filipino," Elizabeth said, like she was trying the word on her tongue. "Is that like China?"

"What do you mean?" I said again.

"Is that a place like China?"

"Uh . . ." I didn't know what to say, because I didn't understand the question.

"Is it an Asian place? Like, China or Japan or . . . whatever?"

"Uh." A few seconds ticked by. "I'm mixed," I said, even though that didn't really answer her question. "I'm half Filipino."

"Oh!" She sounded happy, like she'd just solved a

complicated riddle. "You don't look mixed. You just look . . . you know . . . normal."

"Thanks," I said. But it came out more like a question.

"Your little sister looks like your mom," Elizabeth said. "No offense."

"Oh," I said.

"Tonight was really fun," Elizabeth continued. "Next time we should watch only scary movies. *Really* scary movies."

The next day, I asked my mom if she was Asian or Filipino. She was changing out of her scrubs and into her favorite pajamas. She looked tired. And when I asked the question, she also looked confused.

"I'm both, anak," she said.

"Anak" means "child" in Tagalog, her first language.

"Both?" I said.

"There isn't one way to be Asian," she explained. "There are many different ways. I happen to be Filipino. And you happen to be Filipino, too."

"I don't *look* Filipino," I said. I almost added, *Elizabeth says I look normal.*

But I didn't.

"Maybe I should start planning a trip so you can see where you come from," she said.

So she did.

♀ ♀ ♀

Greta devours her Aloha Pineapple smoothie, but I barely take a sip of mine. I don't want it anymore. Instead, I pinch the straw between my fingers and turn it around and around. Every now and then I sweep my eyes over the food court to see if I can find the Maybe-Friendly Girl, but I don't see her. There are people everywhere. I wonder how many of them think my mom should go back to where she came from. I wonder how many of the kids play Chinese Tag at school.

My mind is turning, just like the straw. I think about the Big Day suitcases. How Greta made sure to clean everything before she packed it in her suitcase, even though it was already clean. How she made sure to include one of her favorite dolls. How carefully she thought about every single item.

And I think about my mom. She works at a nursing home called Restwood. Some of the residents at Restwood don't get visitors, so she makes sure to spend extra time with them. They show her pictures of their families and talk about how proud they are of this grandson or that great-granddaughter, even though they haven't seen them in years. She usually has a favorite resident, like this one old man named Norman Holt. She called him Mr. Norman. Mr. Norman was a Vietnam veteran. He told my mom stories about the war—stories he never told anyone else, mostly because there wasn't anyone around anymore. His family didn't speak to him, and the nurses didn't like him, either. My mother said he could be "very salty," which I thought was a funny expression.

"He must have done something bad if no one wants to talk to him," I said once, when she was talking about Mr. Norman at the dinner table.

"Everyone deserves grace, Camilla," she said. "It's easy to show compassion to people who are kind. Showing compassion to people who aren't—that's the true test."

Test of what? I wondered.

When Mr. Norman died, he left my mother a beat-up cigar box that he'd had since he was a little boy. She showed it to us. It smelled like an old pipe.

"This smells gross," I said. "I'd be mad if someone gave me a smelly box."

My mom took it back and ran her fingers over the top. "This cigar box was the only thing he owned. If you only owned one thing, who would you give it to?"

"Greta," I said without hesitation.

My mother smiled and nodded. "Why Greta?"

"Because she's the most important person to me."

"Exactly," she said.

I don't know why I'm thinking about Mr. Norman

right now as I'm sitting at the table with my mom and Greta and turning the straw in my smoothie around and around. I guess because of those words that woman said. "Hopefully they go back to their own country and stay there."

I bet Mr. Norman wouldn't say that about my mom.

If not for my mom, Mr. Norman's cigar box would have gone straight in the trash.

At that moment, I have a terrible thought. *I hope that lady gets old, and someone puts her in a nursing home and never visits her, just like they did to Mr. Norman. And I hope my mom doesn't work there, because then my mom might keep her company, even if she doesn't deserve it. I hope she's old and bedridden and surrounded by mean nurses who never clean her bedsheets.*

I know it's not a good thing to have in your head, but sometimes my brain thinks not-nice thoughts, especially when I'm mad. And right now I'm mad.

"Hey, Greta?" I say, looking across the table at my sister, who is back on her iPad with an empty smoothie cup in front of her.

She looks up.

"You shouldn't play with Owen Montgomery and them anymore," I say. "They don't sound like very good friends."

Greta doesn't say anything.

"And if you want to keep wearing your disguise, I understand, but I think it's sad that you're hiding your face from the world, because it's a great face. It's an A-plus face, in my opinion."

My mom stops scrolling and raises her eyebrows.

"When you're ready to reveal your true identity, I'll be right here the whole time," I say. "Like your own personal Wolfman. From this point forward, I have wolf-vision. And wolf-ears. So, if anyone wrongs you, I'll be all eyes and ears."

Greta giggles.

"What's in that drink?" my mom says. She picks up my pumpkin smoothie and pretends to investigate it. She exchanges a look with Greta, as if to say, *Who is this girl, and what did she do with Camilla?* "No wonder they call it Jamba Juice."

Greta laughs.

I take a big gulp of my smoothie. Then I move my chair closer to my mother and rest my head on her shoulder.

"Tell us more about Miralinda."

10

Jane

I looked up when I heard the commotion. Everyone sitting at the airport gate did—the woman with the too-long bangs who had been glued to her phone, the guy who had been pouring a bag of chips into his mouth like it was a can of soda, and Gonggong, leaning against the wall, briefly awakened from his now-usual daydreaming stupor. Even Mom stopped waving math flash cards at Annie—but that was only temporary.

"It's nothing, nothing," Mom said, quickly glancing at Gonggong and then flicking her hand at the sounds of confusion as if she could make them disappear. She looked at me. "Go back to studying."

"But I want to know what happened!" Annie bleated, standing and craning her neck. "Why can't we go see?" I couldn't blame her, I wanted to know, too. But Mom frowned at us both and gently, but firmly, pushed Annie back down into her seat.

"Why? It's none of our business," Mom said to her. "Don't get involved in other people's problems."

"Why not?" Annie pouted.

"Because we don't do that kind of thing," Mom said with finality.

A look of rebellion flashed across Annie's face, only to quickly disappear. She couldn't have gone anyway—she was caged in by our rolling suitcases, with Mom as jailer.

Gonggong grunted and moved to a seat that had been abandoned by one of the passengers who had gone to investigate. He mumbled something to Mom, and Annie looked at me. I shrugged. I couldn't understand what Gonggong was saying, either. And it wasn't just because our Taiwanese was so bad. It was because of the accident.

I knew Gonggong would heal and look fine eventually, but right now, just looking at him was painful. The left side of his face was still swollen, especially the deep purple bruise that fanned around his eye in the shape of a plucked butterfly wing. It distorted his eye into a black slanted slit, like those cringy cartoon caricatures of Chinamen. His other eye, the uninjured eye, was harder for me to look at, though. Ever since the accident, that eye was almost always staring dully into space, as he thought of things that he never shared. Though, every once in a while, that eye would look at me. I always had to look away.

But now Gonggong was pulling out his iPad. The man who had been sitting in the seat returned, saw Gonggong, and scowled. But Gonggong didn't even notice him. The iPad blared the music from a Korean soap opera, and the man winced and then rolled his eyes. Mom tapped on Gonggong's knee and handed him his headphones.

"What was it?" the lady with the bangs called out to the annoyed man.

"Dunno," the man said. "Some crazy old Chinese lady trying to smuggle something, I think."

I felt everyone's gaze flick to us and then rest on Gonggong.

"Why's everyone looking at us?" Annie whispered.

"It's nothing," Mom said again. "They don't know we're Taiwanese, not Chinese." She saw me watching as everyone awkwardly glanced away from us, and the low murmur grew into a gossipy chatter. "Jane, keep studying," she admonished me. "We still have another hour before our flight. Don't bother with all this"—she nodded her head in a slight sweeping motion—"junk."

I lowered my head and stared at the workbook that had closed on my lap. *Summer Learning: Getting a Head Start, Grade 7.* The green letters clashed with the bright orange cover, and I could hear my friend Alona's voice. "Your parents make you learn everything before they teach it at school?" she had said with shocked revulsion. "To make sure you get the best grades?" I sighed silently.

I opened the workbook, but as I shifted it on my lap, a small business card fell out of it to the ground. I snatched it up, crushing it in my hand. I quickly looked at Gonggong. He seemed half asleep, staring down at his iPad with his yellow headphones making it look as if his head were growing two lemons. Mom was peppering Annie with addition and subtraction problems that were way too advanced for a first grader, though my sister seemed cheerfully up for the challenge. Annie hadn't been introduced to the cruel, stressful system of grades yet, so she still thought learning was fun.

So, nobody saw the card. I tilted my workbook to hide it and then carefully uncrumpled it. HARRISON DOUGLAS, it said, YMCA REGIONAL MANAGER. I stole a look at Gonggong again. He was definitely asleep now, even though I was pretty sure the soap opera was still blasting into his ears. He looked small and frail. Uncle Jimmy was going to be upset when we got him home to Virginia. We were supposed to bring Gonggong home healthier than before, not worse. I mean, that was the whole reason why Gonggong had come to our area for his foot surgery. "The doctors are better here," Mom had said, "and Dad is a doctor, so he can make sure Gonggong is treated good." Of course, no one had known how long Gonggong would end up staying. What was supposed to be a visit for only a month or two ended up being over a year. Stupid coronavirus.

I looked at Harrison Douglas's business card. *Why don't I just throw this away?* I asked myself, as I had many times before. But, somehow, I just couldn't.

I slipped the card back into my workbook and tried to focus.

According to this text:

A. People are motivated by power.

B. People are motivated by fear.

C. People are motivated by approval.

D. People are motivated by love.

E. People are motivated by justice.

Ugh. I don't know, I thought. I closed my eyes and let my pen choose a letter. "A. People are motivated by power." Power? Was that true? *Maybe if you had some,* I thought wryly. I shook my head. *There should be choice F: All of the above.* But, really, I didn't know if that would be the right answer, either. It seemed like there was no right answer, just like there hadn't been in that fight Gonggong had had with Uncle Jimmy.

That had been months ago, when Gonggong and Mom were having their daily video call with Uncle Jimmy after dinner. Dad was at work, as usual, while Annie and I were in the living room doing schoolwork, leftover stuff from online school. Annie wanted to show off that she could read "real books," even though she was only in kindergarten. She hoped Uncle Jimmy would notice. But he didn't. He was too busy arguing.

"Why you have to do that?" Gonggong had sputtered in his broken English. Uncle Jimmy was a lot younger than Mom and grew up here in the United States, so he didn't speak Taiwanese as well as she did. That meant their conversations were always an odd mixture of Chinese, Taiwanese, and English. I could only usually understand half of what they said.

"Because it was important," Uncle Jimmy shot back. "Do you know what is happening out there? That Black guy was killed! It was murder by the police!"

"You don't know!" Gonggong said, slapping his hand on the table.

"We do know!" Uncle Jimmy said, his voice reminding me of a burning pot—irritated and impatient. "There was a video!"

"Well, I don't understand why you have to go and

march for him," Mom said, "like he was some kind of hero. I saw the news. He was a criminal."

"That's not the point," Uncle Jimmy said. "Police are supposed to arrest people, not kill them."

"But it's got nothing to do with you," Mom said. "Why get involved? You know we don't do that kind of thing."

"Listen, Mei-hua," Uncle Jimmy said to Mom. "We don't, but we should. Because it does have to do with me; it has to do with all of us. Don't you think they look at us differently, too? We have to stand up for Black people when these things happen. We have to stand together."

"No!" Gonggong shot out. "Not our business!" His words were like gunfire that made Mom wince. Then Gonggong said a lot of things in Taiwanese that I didn't quite understand. Something about keeping away from the police? Or just keeping away from trouble? But definitely something about not making problems.

"You think silence is safety!" Uncle Jimmy shouted through the screen. "But saying nothing, doing noth-ing . . . it's the wrong answer!"

That's when Mom stood up and told us to go to our rooms to work.

"What's Uncle Jimmy yelling about, Mommy?" Annie asked as we picked up our stuff.

"Nothing. He just likes to argue with Gonggong,"

Mom said, shaking her head. Then her lips twisted in a weird smile. "Boys are allowed to argue."

"Why?" Annie asked.

"It doesn't matter," Mom said, waving her hands. "He should just listen to Gonggong. All this talking and yelling doesn't change anything. Why bother and make trouble?"

♀ ♀ ♀

"Jane!" Annie's plaintive plea brought me back to the present. I looked at her, pushing at one of our rolling suitcases. "I get a soda now! I finished all the flash cards!"

"How much did *you* do?" Mom asked me. I shrugged. Mom sighed and gave me a couple of bills. "Well, you can catch up on the airplane. Go get Annie a soda. Get a ginger ale or Sprite. No caffeine."

I carefully closed my workbook as Mom maneuvered our luggage so we'd still have the seats when we came back. Annie grabbed my hand and started to skip. "Annie," I groaned at her. "Walk regular!"

"Why?" she asked.

"Because . . . because . . . ," I sputtered, "we don't walk that way."

Annie crumpled. "Just like we don't sing, either?" she said sadly, and dropped into a slow walk.

Then I remembered how Annie had told Mom she

wanted to be a singer when she grew up. But Mom had told her it was impossible. "We're Taiwanese," Mom replied, and then, like she always did, said, "We don't do that kind of thing."

● ● ●

Annie and I walked to the food court. Just as we passed Jamba Juice, I caught someone behind me say, " . . . Asians trying to smuggle something through . . . go back to their own country and stay there."

I couldn't stop myself from turning my head to see who'd said it. A blond lady. In a pink sweater. She wasn't looking at me or Annie, but I couldn't help thinking she was talking about us. I pulled Annie toward McDonald's, almost dragging her across the food court.

"Jane," Annie whined, "slow down. I can't go that fast."

"Sorry," I said, but we were already at McDonald's, so it didn't matter. I looked back toward Jamba. The blond lady was gone.

"Why are people looking at us funny?" Annie said suddenly.

Had she heard the blond lady? But she was looking up at me with curious eyes, without hurt or anger. She hadn't heard. But she was right, of course, about people looking at us. No one in line said anything, but people gave us that quick, guarded glance that I had kind of gotten used to.

"You know," I said to her. "Coronavirus."

"Still?" she said. "It's been a long time."

"Well," I said, "it's probably that Chinese smuggling lady, too."

"What do you think she tried to bring through?" Annie asked me.

"I dunno," I said. "Probably stinky tofu."

Annie laughed. "Maybe it was a thousand-year-old egg!" she said. "Or a durian fruit!"

"Maybe." I smiled, but I started to think. "Though it was a pretty big fuss. It was probably something serious."

"You think maybe it was a gun or a knife or something?" Annie asked, her eyes round with excitement. But then the sparkle dimmed. "But why would an old Chinese lady need something like that?"

I thought of Gonggong's accident and gulped, feeling as if an icy stone had suddenly formed in my throat. "Maybe she felt like she needed some protection," I tried to say lightly. It was time for our order, so I turned away from her. "One small Sprite," I said to the clerk.

As we went back to Mom and Gonggong, we walked past a kid arguing with security about something—I think a guitar? When we walked directly by him, I noticed that he was Asian, too—even though he wore a black rock band

T-shirt that would have made Mom frown. Was he Chinese? Korean? Mom and Gonggong always seemed to be able to tell, but I couldn't. I felt bad for him the way he was arguing with them. *It's not going to do anything*, I wanted to say to him. *Don't bother.*

When we got back to the gate, I saw that our flight was delayed another half hour. I groaned. Gonggong was asleep, making wheezing noises, his headphones still on. The iPad had remained on his lap but was now off, with the cover closed, which I suspected Mom had done. I pushed the suitcase away from my seat while Mom made space for Annie.

"Back to work," Mom said, nodding toward my workbook. "You have another book to get through after this one."

I grimaced. Everyone else I knew spent their summer at camps, or went on vacations filled with beaches and amusement parks with their families. Not me. Every summer was workbooks and studying. Oh, and practicing the piano. School was the vacation.

I opened the workbook again.

What figurative language is used in the following sentence?

He was helpless to do anything, like a goldfish in a bowl watching a cat attack a canary.

The icy stone came back into my throat. *That's how I felt*, I thought. Then, as if on cue, the Harrison Douglas business card slipped onto my lap, showing the back, where a bunch of numbers were written in blue ballpoint ink. *Why don't I just throw this away?* I asked myself again as I clutched the card in my hand. It was like a test question that kept returning, one that I couldn't answer. I wished it would just go away. I wished it would all go away.

But, of course, instead, it just made me remember it all again.

◗◗◗

We had gone to Chinatown. We hadn't been there in a long time, so we were all kind of excited. Gonggong and I decided to go to the bakery while Mom and Annie went to the small grocery store down the street. There were too many people in the bakery, so Gonggong said he would wait outside. I went in and ordered twelve egg tarts, twelve buns (taro, red bean, and lotus seed), a Swiss roll, and a sponge cake.

As the clerk was ringing up my order, I looked back to check on Gonggong. He was leaning against the crosswalk signal light, gazing around leisurely. Both his beige pants and jacket were wrinkled, making him look shabby. But he looked fine—peaceful and content. I was about to turn around to pay, when I saw a man with messy brown hair striding toward the crosswalk.

And then it happened.

The man, the man with the messy hair, raised his arm and slammed it against Gonggong's face.

Gonggong collapsed.

The clerk, a woman with a wide mouth, started pointing and screaming "Aiya! Did you see that?" All the customers turned. Outside, there was more yelling. A woman shrieked and threw her grocery bag, green mangoes rolling on the pavement. A Black man ran across the street shouting, almost getting hit by a car. The man with messy hair sped away.

And I stood frozen, my mouth open, like a gasping goldfish.

But the customers poured out of the bakery, and I found myself moving with them like a leaf caught in a current. They surrounded Gonggong, who was on his knees and bleeding. He peered up at the crowd, saw me, and reached toward me—like Annie when she wants me to open her cheese stick for her. I knelt down. "Gonggong," I whimpered. "Gonggong."

"Here, here!" The clerk from the bakery pushed through with a plastic bag of ice and a towel. The Black man who had run across the street crouched down next to me, the muscles in his arms bulging against his T-shirt sleeves as he rested his elbows on his knees. "This your grandfather?" he asked me. I nodded.

"Should I call an ambulance," he asked, "and the police?"

"*No!*" Gonggong tried to push himself up. Blood was trickling down his face like water on a window during a storm, but his eyes were flashing. "*No police. No one! No!*"

"Easy, easy," the man said. "Okay, I won't call the police."

However, even though the man said he wouldn't call, the word "police" worked its disappearing magic. There was a short fearful murmur, and then the crowd around us seemed to vanish—even the woman who'd thrown her groceries left her mangoes behind. In the span of a moment, it was just me, Gonggong, and the Black man left on the sidewalk.

But the man didn't seem to notice. "Okay, no police," he said to Gonggong, "but how about a doctor? I think you're going to need some stitches there."

"My . . . my dad is a doctor," I stammered. "He'll take care of him."

Gonggong muttered to me in Taiwanese, "Tell him we don't need anything. We'll be fine. Just leave us alone. Tell him to go away and leave us alone."

"My grandfather . . . uh . . . ," I faltered. "He doesn't want you to tell anyone."

The man sighed and then nodded. Then he looked around and swore. "They told us this was happening," he said to the sky, shaking his head, "but I didn't think I'd see it right in front of me.

"Listen." The man looked at me, his gaze so direct that I couldn't look away. His hair, closely cut to his head, looked like velvet, and I could see the soft shine of perspiration on his brow. He stood up and reached into his pocket and wrote something on a small piece of paper. "I work at the YMCA down the street. We were told Asian elderly were getting attacked, and we had this whole seminar about it. I know your grandfather doesn't want police or anything, but there's this hotline where you can report it. They really want to track this stuff so they can stop it."

He handed me the paper, and I could see it was a card, a business card. "That's me, Harrison Douglas," he said. "If he changes his mind, or you want me to report it for you, just call, and I'll do it. Or you can do it yourself. I put down the hotline number and the date and the time of the attack, so you won't forget."

As if I would ever forget.

● ● ●

"Jane!" Annie said, poking me. "I have to go to the bathroom!"

I shook myself from the memories—the slow, hobbling walk to the car while supporting Gonggong; Mom's scream when she saw him, and then her closed, clamped mouth as she nodded at Gonggong's order just to go home; Annie's wet, scared eyes; and Dad stitching Gonggong's cut in the kitchen—all the past images flashing as I turned to Annie.

"What?" I said.

"Jane," Mom said, obviously repeating herself, "take Annie to the bathroom."

Annie pulled me from my seat, but before I stood all the way up, I picked up the business card. *Why don't I throw this away?* I thought again as I put it in my pocket.

All the stalls in the bathroom were full, so Annie and I waited by the sinks. Annie hopped from one leg to the other. "You shouldn't have drunk all that Sprite," I told her.

"Excuse me," a voice said behind me, "my flight leaves really soon. You don't mind if I go ahead of you two, do you?"

I started to nod okay, but as I turned to see who it was, my head froze. It was the blond lady. From in front of Jamba. She smiled sweetly at me, and I could see a pink flake of lipstick on her clenched teeth. Annie squirmed.

"Actually," I said, "we do."

A toilet flushed, and both Annie and I turned around. I felt the blond lady's glare on my back as Annie rushed to the stall. Then another stall opened, and I quickly entered before the blond lady could say anything else. *Why did I do that?* I felt surprised, almost shocked at myself. I knew Mom would've told me to let the blond lady go ahead. We were always supposed to step aside, never make a fuss, always be as invisible as possible. We were never supposed to say no or argue or complain or ask for help—not even when we were attacked on the street. We weren't even supposed to say we were attacked; we had to say it was "an accident," because then there would be fewer questions to answer. Because we didn't answer hard questions at all. We didn't do that kind of thing.

I knew that not letting the blond lady cut in front of us was another thing we didn't do. But I had done it. And when I was alone in the bathroom stall, I felt my mouth curve upward. I wasn't sorry.

◗ ◗ ◗

As Annie and I left the bathroom, we heard a strumming sound. Someone was playing the guitar. "Look, Jane. Look!" Annie said, pointing.

That's when I saw that it was the same guy who had

been talking to security when we had gone to get Annie's soda. That kid who had been arguing about the guitar. I guess he got to keep it after all.

"He plays the guitar. I bet he sings with it, too," Annie said. "Mommy said we don't do that kind of thing. But he does."

"He's probably not Taiwan—" I began, but then I looked at Annie's face, enthralled at her discovery. I stopped. "I guess"—I hesitated—"Mom was wrong."

"Yah!" Annie said. She gazed at the boy as if he were glowing. He looked up and smiled at her.

"Or maybe," I said, biting my lip, "things change."

"Probably that one," Annie said agreeably. "Mommy probably just didn't realize that things are different now."

We turned back to our gate, and I felt strangely light. It was as if that blond lady's glare had burned up a weight that I had been carrying. The business card bulged in my pocket, like forgotten lucky money. All this time, I had kept asking myself why I hadn't thrown it away. Now I knew the answer.

"I can't wait until we get to Virginia," Annie said, "and see Uncle Jimmy."

"Me too," I answered, and I put my hand in my pocket and touched the card. It made me feel weirdly powerful. I grinned, almost giddy. "I'm going to ask him to help me with something."

"Goody," Annie said, and grabbed ahold of my hand. She was skipping again, and this time I skipped with her.

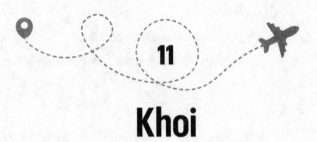

Khoi

"Tôi bị lạc. / I am lost."

"Xin tìm gia đình giúp tôi. / Please help me find my family."

These sentences could come in handy, so I hurriedly write them down in my notepad and dog-ear the page in my Vietnamese phrase book. That's when my dad peeks over my shoulder.

"What are you all stressed out about, kid?"

"Just copying some key phrases, in case I need them on the trip."

"Good thinking, but you should relax. You'll be fine. Though if you're really worried about being in Vietnam for the first time, here's a phrase that'll *actually* be helpful. Repeat after me: Cha tôi rất đẹp trai và thông minh."

"Cha tôi rất đẹp trai và thông minh."

"Great, that'll really impress people."

"What does it mean?"

"My father is very handsome and smart."

I toss the phrase book at my dad and launch what I hope is a devastating side-eye in his direction.

"Dad, you're not helping!"

"What? It's true! I mean, when I was a young man in Vietnam—"

"When your father was a young man in Vietnam," my mom chimes in, "he barely had enough muscle to lift a pair of chopsticks."

"I said I was *handsome and smart*, not strong. Sure, I might have been wiry, but I was actually pretty good at—"

My dad stops when a muffled voice comes over the intercom.

"This is an announcement for Gate B15: Flight 203 to Da Nang has been delayed."

An audible groan courses through the crowd.

"We don't have further details at this time. Please check the monitors regularly for updates. We will provide you with more information as we have it."

I look around and feel the tension of the crowd all throughout the airport. I guess we aren't the only ones being delayed. I wonder if it has anything to do with that commotion in the security line.

I can feel everyone's temperature rising. The airport is like a pot of phở just starting to boil. Except a roiling pot of phở is cause for excitement—the only things bubbling over here are disappointment and anger.

My mom stands up and declares, "I'm getting in line at the desk to find out more."

My dad also leaps into action, announcing, "I'm going to check the monitors to see if they've updated anything yet. Khoi, you stay here and—"

"I'll stay here and watch our stuff, no worries. I'm not going anywhere."

As my parents march off on their scouting mission, I pick up my phrase book again. I open to the back of my notepad where I've been keeping a running list of sentences that I think I might need.

"Tôi không hiểu. / I don't understand."

"Tôi sinh ra ở nước Mỹ. / I was born in the United States."

"Xin lỗi, tôi không nói tiếng Việt. / Sorry, I don't speak Vietnamese."

"Vâng, tôi cũng thất vọng về tôi. / Yes, I'm disappointed in me, too."

It's possible I'm being a little pessimistic about this trip. I flip through the phrase book and decide to add some more helpful sentences.

"Nhà vệ sinh ở đâu? / Where is the bathroom?"

"Xin cho tôi một tô phở? / Can you bring me a bowl of phở?"

"Tôi muốn mua cuốn sách này. Giá bao nhiêu vậy? / I want to buy this book. How much is it?"

That should do it for now. It's not like I'm going to master the entire language on the flight over, even *with* a delay. I close my book and look around the terminal. I actually like airports because they're places of such possibility. People are mostly giddy as they head off to who knows where . . . but when everyone's flights are delayed like this, suddenly that sense of possibility turns to annoyance. We're all stuck here together in this strange world in between home and adventure.

My eyes catch a group of kids over by the food court. I think they're a team of some sort. They're all pretty tall, so maybe a basketball team . . . though everyone seems tall to me, so who knows?

It looks like the delay might be getting to one of them, because he is definitely having words with two bigger teammates. They seem shocked as he lets them have it. This can't end well, so I brace myself (even from a distance I'm allergic to conflict), but then the kid just walks away. He's walking tall and proud—is *that* what it feels like to win an argument? He sees me looking and gives me a little nod.

I, being deeply and eternally awkward, immediately turn away. Maybe someday I'll be cool enough to make eye contact with random people without panicking. But today is not that day. I wish I could be as confident and relaxed as he is . . . instead of sitting over here, worried that I've somehow disappointed an entire country of people who don't even know me.

I flip to a new section of my notepad. If we're going to be here for a while, I might as well be productive. My school is making everyone keep a daily journal of any summer trips and give reports when we get back in the fall.

So that's just great. Not only am I stressed out by this trip, I get the bonus nightmare of having to stand in front of the *whole class* and *talk* about it. My hands are getting clammy just at the thought of it.

But of course I'm going to keep the journal (even the mere idea of skipping an assignment makes me feel ill), so I find a fresh page and start writing.

DAY ONE

Well, this trip has gotten off to a great start. We're stuck at the airport, and they just announced that our flight has been delayed. We have no idea for how long.

If I'm being real, though, part of me is hoping that the flight is totally canceled. And by <u>part of me</u>, I mean pretty much <u>all</u> of me.

Maybe not my stomach, because I was looking forward to good real Vietnamese food, but the rest of me would be totally fine if we had to turn around and go home.

Though, of course, if that happened, I might play it up to my parents and act <u>real disappointed</u>. That way maybe we'd get to go get donuts, and they'd give me extra time to play video games to ease my pain. Of course, if the trip gets canceled, then I won't have to keep this "daily journal," so that's another reason to hope for the airport to call everything off.

Ooh, if they <u>do</u> cancel the flight, I just thought of a great joke to break the news to my parents.

—Knock, knock.

—Who's there?

—Phở.

—Phở who?

—Phở-get about this trip. Let's go to the mall and buy a new video game!

Then we'll all have a big laugh (my parents
love those kind of jokes), and they'll be so
charmed that they'll happily go along with it.
Good plan? No. <u>Brilliant</u> plan.

Hmm . . . that kinda took a weird turn. I don't think
that's the sort of journal entry the school had in mind. I
turn the page and start again.

DAY ONE
At the airport, flight is delayed. Not sure if I
think that's a good thing or a bad thing. Parents
went to find out more details, so we'll see.

I close my notepad and look around. I can see my parents
still trying to get answers (good luck with that), so I have
nothing to do but sit here. I'm tempted to watch something.
I've downloaded three seasons of my favorite show, *Samurai's
Son* (which my grandma calls "Sam Horizon"), but I have *just*
enough episodes to cover the long plane ride to Vietnam. I
calculated it almost down to the minute, and I don't want to
find myself stuck over the Pacific and out of options.

With nothing left to do and nowhere to go, I decide on
my go-to move: NAP.

I stick my arm through my backpack strap and put my feet up on the luggage, so I'll wake up if someone tries any funny business. I'll just close my eyes for a quick minute. . . .

● ● ●

"Time to go, Khoi!"

"What? Huh?"

I sit up with a start to see my parents calling me from down the hallway. I'm foggy, so it's like I'm half dreaming. But I see my parents up ahead carrying their suitcases with them—how did I not wake up when they pulled them from under my feet?

"Time to go, Khoi! Hurry, we have to catch our flight!"

I grab my backpack and start running. My right leg is still asleep (*owww*), but I hobble along, wincing as electricity shoots up my thigh. I have to admit, my parents are pretty fast for old people. I have trouble catching up with them.

It feels like I'm running in quicksand and the hallway is getting longer, but I see them turn a corner, following the sign for customs, so I head that way. I thought my parents said we wouldn't have to deal with customs until we arrived in Vietnam. So, this is great: another curveball.

When I round the corner, I run into a horde of people waiting to get through the customs line. I scan the crowd for my parents . . . and . . . they've already made it past the checkpoint and are standing in a hallway through a set of glass doors.

"Mom! Dad! Why didn't you wait for me? Why didn't you wake me up sooner?"

But they're too far away to hear. I have no choice but to make my way through the line.

I shuffle along impatiently. Can't this line move any faster? A voice comes in overhead: "Please proceed in an orderly fashion. Remain calm, and everything will go more smoothly."

Thanks a lot, intercom lady. I try to glare at everyone in line to make them move faster. No one makes eye contact with me, which is lucky for them, because I am shooting daggers out of my sockets.

I finally make it to the front of the line (thanks for nothing, Mom and Dad), and I walk up to the security officer at the podium.

"Con đi đâu?"

OHHH CRAAAP.

"Oh, sorry, umm . . . Tôi không . . . Việt . . . gahh. I don't speak Vietnamese. I only speak English."

"Tại sao con không nói tiếng Việt?"

"Wait, hold on, let me get my phrase book out real quick. . . ."

The guard glowers at me as I riffle through my bag, but I can't find my phrase book or notepad in all the mess. The line behind me is getting restless, so I panic and just grasp for the first phrase that comes to mind.

"Cha tôi rất đẹp trai và thông minh!"

The guard looks at me with a mix of confusion and disgust. He switches to English.

"I don't care if your father is good-looking and smart. You still have to fill out these forms."

The guard shoves a clipboard with a thick stack of papers on it at me. He marches me to a nearby seat and hands me a pen.

"My parents are already through. Can I just—"

But the guard has already left me and gone back to his post.

I sit down with the clipboard, which says *Customs* in large, bold letters across the top. My parents warned me about customs before the trip. We just have to declare any unusual items we might have packed away. I only have my bag, and I'm not bringing any fruits, vegetables, or exotic creatures on the plane with me, so hopefully I can just breeze through these forms—

OH NO.

Vietnamese Customs Question #1: What is the name of

the Buddhist holiday that celebrates parents, and what day is it?

WHAT THE—This can't be right . . . but the whole page is filled with questions like this. I flip to the middle of the packet and pick another random question.

Vietnamese Customs Question #658: You enter a room and see your parents, their childhood friends, an older couple about eighty-five years old (whom you don't know), and a monk.
    Whom do you address first?
    How do you refer to them?
    Do you refer to yourself in the first person, third person, or not at all?
    Do you bow, and if so, how deeply?

GAAAAHHHH. I can't answer these questions on my own! I stand and look for my parents, but they are still too far ahead of me to help. I open to another page, hoping for an easier question.

Vietnamese Customs Question #1,713: You are having dinner at your grandmother's house. You have finished two rounds of food already, and you are totally full. She goes to fill your bowl again. Do you:

    a.   Say thank you but decline because you are full.

    b.   Lay your chopsticks over your bowl to signal that you're done.

    c.   Say yes and just do your best to keep eating.

    d.   Say yes for eternity and keep eating until you end up in the hospital.

    e.   Run away screaming, never to return.

My collar is hot around my neck, and my palms are clammy with panic. I look past the guard to the other side of the glass, where my parents are waiting to board the plane. But now they aren't alone.

Next to them I see my mom's parents (my ông bà ngoại) and some uncles and aunts gathering around. Then I see others, ancestors who died long ago, whom I recognize from old photographs and paintings. Many are dressed in traditional Vietnamese áo dài; all of them are staring at me, waiting for me to come through.

I have no idea what is going on, but I somehow know that I am going to disappoint them.

I might as well just give up: there is no way this is going to turn out well.

I put the clipboard down and pick up my backpack.

Looking out on the sea of strangers that fills the airport,

I want to just disappear into the crowd.

I turn back for one last look at my family. They are all still standing there on the other side of the glass. Nothing has changed . . . and yet, as I scan these faces, my parents, my grandparents, all the ancestors, they don't look disappointed, just . . . nervous and hopeful.

My grandmother's eyes lock onto mine, anxiously waiting to see what I'm going to do next, and suddenly I'm not ready to walk away.

I push my way through the crowd and stand up to the security guard. I nervously clear my throat and, carefully and deliberately, say: "Tôi bị lạc."

"You are lost?"

"Yes . . . Tôi bị lạc. Xin tìm gia đình giúp tôi."

"Of course I can help you find your family. Why didn't you just say so before?"

I let out the breath I had been holding as he leads me back to the glass hall. I can see my parents and all the other family members and ancestors smiling as I head their way.

They start to board the plane as the guard opens the door.

I walk through and pause in the doorway as a wave of relief washes over me.

I made it.

I look up, and most of the family has started boarding.

My parents are standing at the door of the plane, waving and calling for me to come join them.

"Time to go, Khoi!"

I smile and excitedly head toward them.

"Time to go, Khoi!"

I feel light on my feet. I'm practically flying and can't wait to get on the plane.

"Time to go, Khoi!"

● ● ●

I wake with a start. I look around. I'm still at Gate B15. The airport crowd still feels disgruntled. That basketball team is still huddled around the food court.

"Time to go, Khoi!"

My parents are standing above me, gathering their bags.

"Time to go. They just changed our gate to one on the other side of the terminal. Let's head that way now so we can get a good spot."

How long was I asleep? I rub my face and chest with my hands. This all feels real. . . .

"Are we headed to customs?"

"What? No, customs is when we get *to* Vietnam, remember? Now, hurry and let's get going!"

We grab our stuff. My parents roll off with their luggage as I throw my backpack on and follow. My leg is asleep, so

I kind of hobble after them. I get about fifteen feet when I feel someone tug on my backpack. I turn around.

It's one of the basketball players from the food court. He's smiling at me. It's that same confident smile he had on his face earlier when he walked away after that fight.

"Sorry, I didn't mean to scare you, but you forgot this."

He hands me my Vietnamese phrase book.

"Oh, hey, thanks . . .

"No problem. My name's AJ. First trip back to the motherland, huh?"

"Is it that obvious?"

"Kinda. My first trip back to the Philippines, I was a total mess, too. I even had a book like this, but for Tagalog."

"Yeah? And how was the trip?"

"Best trip of my life."

"Really? Even though you couldn't speak that well?"

"Yup . . . I think you'll find that some things are just deeper than words. Trust that, and you'll be fine."

"Wow, I hope you're right . . . but I should go. I don't want my family to leave me behind."

"I don't think you have to worry about that."

AJ points over my shoulder. I look down the hall to see my parents gesturing wildly for me to follow them.

"*Khoi*, come on, let's *go*! Keep up so you don't get lost!"

"Ha, I gotta run. Thanks for the book!"

"Have a great trip, man!"

I say bye to AJ and hurry toward my parents. I finally reach them as we step onto one of those moving sidewalks. Then we have a chance to catch our breath for a minute.

"Hey, I have a question. . . . In Vietnam, if there are a lot of people in a room, how do I know who to greet first?"

"Ha, that is always a tricky question," my mom responds. "I still have problems with that, too . . . but it's a long flight, and we'll have plenty of time to talk about traditions and customs on the plane!"

We step off the moving walkway and scurry down the hall to our new gate. My parents are still frazzled, looking on their phones, eyes darting all over, checking the flight information on the overhead monitors.

As we wait, I pull out my notepad and open to my daily journal entry.

DAY ONE (CONTINUED)

Fell asleep in airport. Had a wild (kind of terrifying) dream. But it turned out okay in the end, and I actually—surprise!—managed to speak a little Vietnamese in the dream. So that kinda feels like progress?

We're waiting again. And I'm realizing now

that I'm hoping for the flight to start boarding. I'm actually not rooting for everything to be canceled anymore.

So, fingers crossed that we take off soon—and that my next journal entry will be from Vietnam.

Then I flip a few pages in my notepad and check my phrase book to add a few new sentences to my list:

"Tên tôi là Khoi. / My name is Khoi."

"Tôi rất vui được ở đây. / I'm excited to be here."

12

Soojin

Soojin Yoo glared at the directory. On the map, the airport was a sprawling complex with numerous concourses branching out from the main terminal like long, curving spider legs. There were many stores scattered throughout the airport, even luxury brand names found in high-end shopping malls, but Soojin's eyes were fixed on the one little circle that said, *You are here.*

She didn't want to be here.

In an airport.

In Chicago.

They'd just gotten off a plane from New York to transfer to their fourteen-hour flight to Seoul, and her mother scoured the map as she muttered, "Gate B17." Eomma asked Soojin to help look for the gate, but Soojin ignored her. She kept staring at the little circle.

"I am here, but not for long," Soojin whispered as she traced the circle with her finger. She leaned her head to rest it on the cool glass surface of the display.

"I don't want to move to Korea," she said loudly.

Her mother ignored her statement, just as she'd done all week.

"Here it is!" Eomma exclaimed. "Why do they make it so far away? So much walking." She turned to face Soojin and smiled. "The food court is in the middle. Let's go eat first."

Soojin could see the conciliation offered in her mother's eyes, but Soojin was not ready to forgive her. She didn't know if she ever would be, given that Eomma had declared the two of them would move to Seoul—and leave Soojin's father behind in New York City.

While Soojin was used to hearing her parents argue, their fight last week was the worst of her entire life. It had started with the break-in at their store. The robbers had stolen everything they could take and destroyed all that was left. To make matters worse, they'd scrawled racist graffiti inside and outside the store. On the sidewalk, they'd sprayed "Go back to China." That was the final insult for her mother.

"They don't want us here! Let's go home," Eomma had *pleaded with Appa.*

"This is our home," Appa had replied.

"Maybe for you," Eomma had said. "But not for me. And not for Soojin."

And just like that, Soojin was moving back to Korea. It didn't matter that Soojin loved America and didn't want to move. New York was her home. It hurt that Eomma could not understand this important fact, but the hardest part was Soojin's father's reaction. When her mother said Soojin was coming with her, he'd just agreed—because he blamed himself for their troubles.

Appa had wanted to come to America to start his own business. He'd tried so hard to get a good job in South Korea, but as a poor graduate student with no connections, he failed to pass initial interviews for the corporate jobs he'd dreamed of. Meanwhile, Soojin's mom was the daughter of a well-to-do family from Seoul. She probably wouldn't have worked a day of her life if she hadn't fallen in love with Soojin's father. Her dad said he was the root of all their problems, but Soojin thought the problems lay squarely with her mother. Eomma never wanted to live in America in the first place.

She side-eyed her mom critically. Eomma was a beautiful woman who kept her long black hair in a tight ponytail and was dressed impeccably in gray slacks and a sleeveless white top with a matching white cardigan. She was always so elegant. Even when they'd be busy restocking shelves, her mother looked as if she was going to a fancy brunch. She had always appeared out of place in their store.

"Let's go, Soojin," Eomma said. She turned to leave when her large carry-on bag bumped into a short white man standing in the gate area.

"Excuse me," she said.

The man scowled at her and then looked at Soojin in disgust.

"Nobody can hear you through those filthy masks," he grunted.

Soojin's teeth clenched as she felt a wave of heat flush through her. But before she could respond, her mother was apologizing and pulling her away quickly.

"Jerk," Soojin muttered under her breath.

"Soojin," her mother admonished. Unspoken was the demand: *Don't make a scene. Don't bring undue attention. Don't cause trouble.*

Soojin adjusted her heavy black backpack and trailed behind her mother as they moved into the large hall linking the gates to the rest of the terminal.

A huge crack of thunder startled her. Glancing up at the floor-to-ceiling glass windows behind the information counters, Soojin realized that the bad weather they had flown through had gotten a lot worse. Many of the flight information screens were flashing "delayed" or "canceled."

Soojin tugged at her mother's arm. "We'd better check on our flight," she said.

With a gasp of alarm, her mother rushed over to a row of information screens. Soojin trailed behind her, noting two security guards talking to a young boy carrying a little girl in a yellow dress and light-up shoes.

Soojin overheard the boy say he was trying to take the little girl back to her family. But when one of the security guards tried to pick up the girl, she shook her head vehemently, slapping the boy in the face with her pigtails and hugging him even tighter.

It was so funny and cute. Their interaction reminded Soojin of Rachel Watkins, her favorite customer and friend. When Soojin's parents first opened up their grocery and delicatessen in Queens, ten-year-old Rachel had made it her mission to help four-year-old Soojin learn English quickly. Rachel not only taught her to read, she also played with her, giving her piggyback rides and braiding her hair. Rachel was the older sister that Soojin had always wanted. Soojin looked down at her thick purple NYU hoodie—a present from Rachel. Now that her friend was attending NYU, Soojin was determined to go there also.

But moving back to Korea meant she wouldn't see Rachel anymore. And NYU was probably just a dream.

Soojin fingered the raised letters of her sweatshirt and swallowed back a bitter sigh.

"Oh, thank goodness!" her mother said. "The earlier flight to Seoul was canceled, but ours was just delayed three hours."

Frustration and anger warred inside of Soojin. But the worst feeling was her absolute sense of helplessness.

"I hate this airport," Soojin seethed.

"Sorry, honey," her mother said, looking at her daughter guiltily. "You must be in a bad mood because you're hungry."

Soojin rolled her eyes so hard, they hurt. No, she wasn't hungry at all, but she marched down the corridor toward the food court anyway.

Reaching an empty table, Soojin plopped herself into a chair and yanked off her purple mask. Her mother placed her large carry-on bag on the table and began pulling out small margarine, sour cream, and cream cheese containers that were filled with delicious Korean side dishes: myeolchi bokkeum, crisp little anchovies in a sweet-and-salty marinade; hobak jeon, battered and fried zucchini; and Soojin's favorite: gyeran mari, rolled eggs mixed with scallions, carrots, and ham. As her mother opened each container, Soojin slouched deeper in her seat, scowling down at the table.

"What the heck are they eating?" someone nearby whispered.

Soojin abruptly sat up and glared at the kids sitting at the next table. A little boy and girl, younger than her—maybe seven or eight—were devouring burgers and fries while their mother was busy feeding a messy, shrieking toddler.

"Ew, what's that black stuff?"

"Is that sushi?"

"Raw fish? Ew!"

Soojin's mother had unrolled kimbap that had been wrapped in aluminum foil. She handed Soojin a pair of chopsticks.

"I'll go get some water," her mother said. "You start eating."

Usually seeing a spread of her favorite foods would put Soojin in a good mood. But it was hard to be hungry when your world was falling completely apart.

"Why isn't she eating?" the little girl asked.

"Maybe it's gross even for her," the little boy responded. They both giggled.

Those kids are so annoying, Soojin thought.

Gritting her teeth, she snapped her chopsticks apart, speared a round piece of kimbap, and shoved it in her mouth. Turning to face the nosy kids, she said, "Mmm, delicious. Homemade food is so much better than greasy fast food."

The kids stared down at their meals.

"Soojin!" Her mother stood next to her, two filled water bottles in her hands. "Don't be rude."

"They were the ones saying mean things about our food," Soojin replied. "I was just stating facts."

The kids' mother suddenly said, "I'm sorry, were the twins being rude? Josh, Meg, apologize right now."

The kids apologized so politely that Soojin was forced to accept it or look like a jerk. She gave them a nod of acceptance and turned back to her lunch.

"I'm Lori, by the way," the twins' mother said as she leaned over to peer at their kimbap. "Oh, that looks so delicious! What is it?"

Eomma explained what it was and offered some kimbap to the twins and their mom. Raving about how wonderful it was, Lori began asking questions about how to make it, and soon the two moms were sharing recipes.

Soojin tuned them completely out as the food sat like lead in her stomach. She wondered what her father was doing. Appa had vowed to reopen the store, but her mother had asked how he would do so with their inventory gone and no insurance.

"I'll borrow some money," Appa had said.

"Again? We just paid off the first loan," Eomma said.

"And we can repay this one also," Appa replied. "We can rebuild this. . . ."

"No. I'm tired. I can't do this anymore."

"Then I'll do it myself," Appa said. "Don't worry. You can go stay with your parents and rest. I will work really hard for our family. And then you and Soojin can come back to me."

"What if we don't want to come back?" Eomma had said.

Soojin shoved another piece of kimbap in her mouth. A painful hiccup caught in her throat, and she quickly opened her water bottle. As she took a long sip, a well-dressed white couple seated themselves at the table next to her.

"TSA is such a joke," the man grumbled. "Can't believe they shut down the line over a can of coffee."

"It wasn't coffee, Chad. Get your facts right. It was human remains in a can," the woman remarked. "Absolutely disgusting. Seriously, who puts their husband's ashes in a coffee can?"

"What do you expect from foreigners?" Chad sniffed as he frowned contemptuously at Soojin and her mother. "No manners."

Soojin blinked in shock. Why was he staring at them? Was he calling them foreigners with no manners? Soojin slammed her water bottle on the table and gave Chad the stink eye.

"Don't do that, Soojin," Eomma said in Korean. "We don't want to cause any trouble."

The white woman suddenly turned to them and said in a loud mocking voice, "Speak English! This is America."

Soojin felt a surge of anger, but she could clearly read her mother's expression. *Don't make a scene*, it said.

Soojin's eyes narrowed as she glared at her mother. Soojin couldn't let it go. She was too upset. Her urge to confront the woman battled with years of training to be a dutiful daughter.

Eomma's expression sharpened.

Soojin bit her lip. As angry as she was with her mother, she would not defy her. But she still would not back down.

She swallowed her angry retort and kept her tone light. "Okay, sure, we can speak English if you want," Soojin responded. "We also speak Korean, and my mother is fluent in Mandarin and Japanese as well. How many languages do you speak?"

The woman's smug expression faded while Chad looked thunderous.

"English is the only language of importance," he said haughtily.

Soojin assumed an expression of mock sympathy. "Oh, I see. You only speak English," she replied. "I'm so sorry. How sad for you. I'm only twelve, and I speak two languages. I'm even learning Spanish in school. Too bad you only speak one."

An older white couple sitting a table away called out, "That's right, little lady! What kind of ignoramus says something so ridiculous? You ought to be ashamed of yourself, young man!"

The twins' mom chimed in. "I'm fluent in French, and my children are enrolled in a French immersion program at school. Why would anyone think that English is the only important language?"

At their mother's words, Josh and Meg loudly showed off their French in such a deliberately obnoxious manner that Soojin had to smile. Maybe the twins weren't so bad after all.

Apparently, the roasting by little kids was too much for Chad. He shoved his food back into his paper bag and stood up. "Come on, Donna, let's get out of here."

Soojin chuckled as the twins said goodbye in several different languages. Lori winked at her. "What can I say? My kids watch a lot of PBS."

She turned her attention back to her exuberant toddler, who was now throwing french fries to the ground.

Soojin caught her mother looking at her strangely. "What's the matter, Eomma?"

Her mother shook her head. "Nothing. I just expected

you to yell at them and cause trouble. Instead, you called them out, and everyone was on your side. I guess you're more like your father than me. Everybody always likes your father."

Soojin tilted her head as she looked at her mom. She loved her father, but she didn't think being likable was why people had sided with her. "No, it's not that. It's because I'm American. I spoke up."

"But you're not American, you're Korean," Eomma replied. "Don't ever forget that."

Soojin sucked in a breath. Her mother's words cut her deep.

"I would never forget that I'm Korean, Eomma," Soojin said quietly. "But I'm also American. I've lived here longer than in Korea. You can't forget that, either."

Eomma fiddled with her chopsticks. With a deep sigh, she put them down and folded her hands. "For me, coming from Korea, the racism against Asians here has been very hard," she said.

"It's hard for me, too," Soojin responded. "But I still love America. I love being a New Yorker. Appa always says there are more good people than bad in the world. And instead of thinking about the terrible things, you've got to remember all the good ones. Appa says thinking about only the bad things will make you unhappy." Soojin gave her mother a pointed look.

Eomma smoothed her hair back as she paused for a long moment. "It's not just about me being unhappy. I hate that you've had to spend your childhood in a store, helping me and your appa, when you should be out playing with your friends and not worrying about our business. What kind of life has this been for you?"

"I don't mind," Soojin said. "I have good friends. I like my school. I like helping in the store. I like most of our customers."

"This is not what I wanted for you."

"But, Eomma, why can't you believe that I'm happy?"

Eomma didn't respond, and they both sat silently. After a moment, Eomma stood up. "I need some coffee. I'll be right back."

Soojin gazed around the food court. It was crowded with people coming in and out, looking for a place to sit. There were families wearing red, white, and blue to celebrate the Fourth of July. Soojin had almost forgotten it was the holiday weekend. Last year, her father had closed the store early and taken them to Long Island City to watch the Macy's fireworks over the East River. It had been worth the long wait to see the most spectacular fireworks display of her entire life. This year she wouldn't even be able to watch them on television.

Her eye was caught by two girls sitting at a table with an Asian woman. The younger girl had a dark blue cap pulled low over her face and was busy on an iPad; the older girl was wearing a burgundy T-shirt that said *Texas A&M*. Soojin watched as the older one leaned over to say something to the younger girl, making her giggle and put down her iPad. The interaction made Soojin think of Rachel again. Of how much she'd miss her honorary big sister.

Eomma returned with a cup of hot water. She took out a narrow yellow pouch labeled *Maxim Mocha Coffee Mix*, poured it into her cup, and stirred it up. Soojin knew Eomma drank instant coffee because it was cheap. Because she was saving money. A sliver of guilt tickled at Soojin. Her father had given her a twenty-dollar bill to spend on anything she wanted. She could buy her mother a nice coffee and still have enough for a treat for herself. But the money was a gift from Appa, and Soojin wanted to spend it on something special that was just for her.

The twins suddenly appeared at Soojin's side, shoving a large bag of popcorn in her face.

"You want some?" Meg asked.

The bag was full of orange and brown kernels and had a big blue label across it that said *Garrett*.

Soojin stared in surprise. Up close, the orange of the kernels was like the color of Cheetos, and the brown ones reminded her of Cracker Jacks. "Is that cheese- and caramel-flavored popcorn mixed together?" she asked.

The twins nodded enthusiastically as they shoved handfuls into their mouth. "It's our favorite! You've got to try it!" Josh said. Grabbing the bag from his sister, he poured the mix into Soojin's hands. "You gotta eat them together!"

Soojin was grossed out by the flavor combination, but the twins were being very nice, and Soojin felt guilty for having been mean to them earlier.

"Okay, thanks," she said as she selected one cheddar and one caramel kernel and cautiously placed them both into her mouth. The combination of sweet and salty flavors exploded on her taste buds.

"Wow!" Soojin exclaimed in shock. "That's delicious!"

The twins beamed in delight.

"Told you!" Josh crowed.

Soojin inhaled the rest of the popcorn. She needed more. "Where can I buy some?" she asked.

"There's a stand right outside the food court," the twins' mother replied. "Garrett is a Chicago institution. You should get some before you go."

Soojin nodded enthusiastically. Reaching into her

backpack, Soojin pulled out the twenty-dollar bill her father had given her. "Eomma, Appa told me to get whatever I want," Soojin said. "I want to get a bag of Garrett popcorn to take with us on the plane."

Her mother looked surprised. "You really like it?"

Soojin nodded. It was hard to describe the taste. Sweet, salty, buttery: an impossible combination that was unexpectedly and utterly delicious.

"It tastes like America," Soojin responded wistfully.

Eomma frowned, and Soojin wondered what she'd said this time to upset her mother. Shrugging it off, she put on her mask and began to clear the table. After saying goodbye to the twins, Soojin recycled their containers and waited impatiently for her mother so they could find the popcorn stand. As they walked toward the end of the food court, they stepped around a group of boys in matching red-and-white basketball warm-ups with *Perez, DDS* logos. Soojin couldn't help but gawk at them. A few of them caught her staring and began to pose, like models. It was so funny, Soojin had to laugh. Between the excitement of buying popcorn and the goofy behavior of the basketball players, Soojin's mood lightened considerably.

As she passed into a less crowded area, she heard a voice yell, "*Khoi*, come on, let's *go*! Keep up so you don't get lost!" A cute boy came running over to a couple waiting at the start of a moving sidewalk. They stepped onto the conveyor belt together, the father affectionately ruffling his son's hair.

Soojin wished her father was with her. She knew he would have been just as excited as she was to buy Garrett popcorn. New things made them both happy.

Then she spotted the blue-striped sign that read *Garrett Popcorn Shops, A Chicago Tradition*. The aroma of buttery popcorn lifted her spirits further as she hurried toward the stand. She waited on line eagerly, watching customers buy bags of brown-and-orange joy. The man at the front of the line bought two large tins full of Garrett Mix, and for a moment, Soojin worried that they would run out. She was relieved to see a worker refilling the popcorn bins. She gazed wistfully at the too-costly tins and memorized the menu. When it was her turn, she knew exactly what to order.

"May I have a large Garrett Mix, please?" Soojin asked.

The pretty Latina woman behind the counter wore a mask, but her eyes were kind as she rang her up. "Excellent choice," she said.

Eomma gasped at the price. "Omo, Soojin, that's so expensive," she said.

Soojin tightened her lips as she handed over the money. "It's worth it."

The cashier winked at her, and her eyes crinkled as if she was smiling. "I'm so glad to hear you say that," she said to Soojin as she handed her the large bag of brown and orange popcorn. "There are some people who think it's weird."

Soojin nodded. "I just tried it today, and I love it!"

"Hey, a new convert!" The cashier laughed. "Welcome to our club! I hope you enjoy it, and please come back to see us again!"

Hugging her bag of popcorn, Soojin inhaled the warm, sweet, buttery-and-cheesy smell with a happy sigh. "I wish Appa was here, so he could share this with me," she said. "I bet he would love it, too."

Her mother was silent, as she always was when Soojin mentioned her father. Then she said, "We still have several hours. Let's go sit at a table again."

Soojin followed her mother down the hall and back toward the open seating area. From the corner of her eye, Soojin saw the little pigtailed girl in the yellow dress again. Her light-up shoes flashed as she held her mother's hand and walked by. Something about the girl reminded Soojin of herself and that first time flying into the US. She remembered holding her father's hand tightly and the stern-looking customs officer who scared her until he smiled and shook her hand, saying, "Welcome to America."

Soojin watched as the little girl turned around to wave at a boy wearing a black baseball cap who trailed behind her with an older lady in a lime-green puffy coat.

That must be her family, Soojin thought. *That nice kid was able to reunite them. Probably because of that coat.*

Soojin giggled. That coat would be hard to miss.

"What's so funny?" Eomma asked.

Soojin gestured toward the family. "It's like a hundred degrees outside, and that grandma is wearing a winter coat."

Just as Eomma turned to look, an angry blond woman wearing a bright pink sweater and towing a boy who looked a lot like her stormed up to the grandmother.

"We missed our plane because of your illegal activities, and now there are no more flights to Burlington today, and this nightmare is going to cost me a small fortune!" the woman yelled. "This is all your fault! What are you going to do about it?"

The black-capped boy stepped in front of his grandmother as if to protect her, while the parents interceded.

"Look, it's not our fault that you didn't come to the airport earlier," the little girl's mother stated. "That's on you."

As the adults argued, Soojin noticed the blond son

stick out his tongue at the brother and sister and then pull both his eyes back into tight slits. The little girl, standing with her brother, began to cry.

Soojin froze. On the brother's face, she could see the same anger and hurt that filled her. Soojin saw the frightened confusion on the little girl's face, and she remembered the first time another child had done the same thing to her. She'd been so confused. It had felt mean and terrible, even though she hadn't understood why. And when she finally did understand, it had hurt even more.

Those memories compelled her to go forward, her thoughts focused on how the little girl must be feeling. She wanted to help.

"Soojin, where are you going?" Eomma asked.

Ignoring her mom, Soojin came up to the kids and stepped between the blond boy and the little girl. Turning her back on him, she knelt in front of the girl.

"Hey, don't pay any attention to the rude jerk." Tugging her mask down under her chin so the girl could see her smile, Soojin said, "Do you want to try something new?" She opened her popcorn bag. "I'd never even heard of Garrett Mix before today, and I love it."

The little girl's eyes grew wide, and she stopped crying as Soojin poured some into her hands.

"What kind of idiot has never heard of Garrett pop-corn?" the blond boy sneered.

Soojin stood up but ignored his question. She watched as the little girl delicately nibbled at a few kernels. "It's good, isn't it?"

"*It's good, isn't it?*" the blond boy repeated in a high, mocking voice. "What a loser."

Soojin could see the girl's brother's growing agitation. She cupped her hand around her ear and frowned. Then she winked at the brother. "Did you hear something?" she asked him. "I thought I heard something weird."

He grinned. "Nah, I didn't hear anything."

"Hey!" the blond boy squawked, stepping closer. "I'm talking to you!"

"There's that weird sound again," Soojin said, rolling her eyes.

The boy flushed angrily. "Hey, look at me when I talk to you!" he said, and he slapped at the bag of popcorn in Soojin's hand. Brown and orange kernels flew everywhere.

"My popcorn!" Soojin cried.

The girl hid her face behind her brother's leg as he cried, "What's wrong with you?"

The blond boy smirked. "Whatcha gonna do about it?"

For a moment, Soojin stared down at the now empty

bag blankly. And then all the pent-up emotions that she'd been holding in all week finally erupted into an anger greater than any she'd ever experienced before. She was done playing nice. This time she would not hold back. This time, she would make a scene.

Stepping toward the boy, Soojin let her anger free. "That was a horrible thing to do, and you're an awful boy! You owe me a new bag of Garrett Mix!"

"I don't owe you nothing!" he replied defiantly. But his eyes shifted, as if in guilt.

"Look what you did!" Soojin gestured angrily at the mess on the floor. "Does it make you feel good, being so nasty?"

The blond boy didn't respond. His eyes darted around as he realized Soojin's words had drawn a crowd of people around them.

Now the attention of the feuding adults turned to them, and the blond woman imposed herself in front of her son.

"Leave him alone," she said sharply.

"He spilled all my popcorn!" Soojin yelled.

"That's your problem," the woman retorted.

"Actually, it's your responsibility as his parent," a tall white man said as he stepped up to stand next to Soojin, giving her a reassuring look. "I mean, we all saw him hit her."

Confronted by the tall stranger, the woman tried to laugh it off. "They're just kids fooling around."

"Dad, shouldn't we call security?" a girl called out to him, standing with another man who had his hands on her shoulders. Soojin thought the girl and the men looked familiar and then remembered them from her earlier New York flight.

"Good idea, Min. Not only did her son hit the young girl, but this lady is clearly harassing this poor family." The man turned to the grandmother. "I'm a reporter for the *New York Times*. Would you like to tell me what spurred this attack?"

"I remember you from before. You have no idea what you're talking about! Stop it!" the blond woman yelled, her face flushing a deep, splotchy red.

"We saw the whole thing and recorded it," shouted a brown-haired girl, who stood arm in arm with a girl wearing a perfect *Kiki's Delivery Service* red bow.

The woman seemed shocked to see so many people frowning disapprovingly at her. Bystanders started calling out:

"You ought to be ashamed of yourself!"

"Leave the poor family alone!"

"You owe that little girl money!"

Soojin noticed that the people scolding the woman

were not just Asians. They were all races, and they were united in one thing: they didn't like bullies.

"There seems to be a misunderstanding," the woman said finally with a weak smile. "We have to leave now."

Grabbing her son's arm, the woman stomped off to the sound of jeers and cheers.

"Hey, I'm sorry about your popcorn," the black-capped boy said. "What a messed-up thing to do."

Suddenly, his mother called him over. "Paul, honey, can you come here and explain to this nice man what happened at TSA?"

They both glanced over to see the reporter trying to communicate with Paul's grandmother, who was gazing at him suspiciously.

"If you don't mind," the reporter said, "I'd love to walk you to your gate and chat with you about what happened."

Paul sighed and turned back to Soojin.

"I have to go now. Are you okay?"

Soojin nodded and said goodbye to him and his sister before squatting on the floor, attempting to clean up the spilled popcorn. Her mother came over and dropped her travel bag on a clean space of floor nearby.

"What a terrible thing to do," Eomma said as she knelt by her side. "But all those other people stepped up to help you, just like in the food court." Eomma sounded thoughtful as she swept kernels onto some napkins. Soojin rocked back on her heels and surveyed the area, noting how far the kernels had traveled and what a mess they made as people crushed them under their feet.

"I don't think we can clean this all up." Soojin sighed.

As if she'd heard Soojin's words, a white woman with a purple-streaked ponytail pushing a large cleaning-supply cart waved at them. She was wearing an airport uniform with a name tag that said ANGIE.

"You don't have to do that," Angie said. She took the trash from their hands gently, threw it in the garbage, then pulled a broom out of her cart. "I'll take care of it. Don't worry."

Eomma stood up and thanked the woman.

"I saw what happened, and I'm so sorry," Angie said sympathetically. Then she turned to Soojin. "They should have bought you a new bag of Garrett Mix!"

Soojin shrugged. "It's okay," she replied.

But it wasn't. The emotions that had been raging through her system were draining away now, leaving an exhausted stillness behind them. Soojin felt empty and alone.

Saying goodbye to Angie, Eomma led her daughter to

a table to sit down at again.

"I think I need more coffee." Eomma sighed.

Taking out the remainder of her money, Soojin handed it to Eomma. "Here, I don't need it anymore. You can have it."

"Don't you want another bag of popcorn?" Eomma asked, hesitating.

Soojin shook her head, staring down at the table. She didn't respond when her mother asked if she wanted anything else. Nothing mattered anymore.

"There must be something you want, Soojin?" Eomma asked.

"The only thing I want is to go home," Soojin said in a dull voice. She didn't look up when her mother stepped away. Soojin was filled with a sadness she couldn't shake.

At a nearby gate, a boy sat alone, playing electric guitar. Soojin didn't recognize the song, but the sound was unexpectedly soothing. She noticed a little girl watching the guitar player in awe, as if he was a rock star, before skipping off with her sister.

After a few minutes, he packed up his guitar, grabbed his bag, and walked down the hallway. Soojin watched him leave, admiring the fact that he was traveling on his own. He seemed confident and happy about where he was headed, unlike Soojin.

There was a dull aching pain in the middle of Soojin's chest.

Eomma came back with a small cup of coffee and a chocolate chip cookie that she gently laid in front of Soojin. Ignoring it, Soojin picked at the hem of her NYU sweatshirt, where a few crumbs of Garrett Mix clung to the purple fabric. She rubbed a tiny piece of cheese popcorn and a caramel kernel together between her fingers, wondering when she would ever taste the unique flavor again. Tears slipped down her cheeks.

"Soojin, why are you crying?" Eomma asked softly.

Unable to speak, Soojin put her head down on the table.

"You hate the idea of going to Korea this much?" her mother asked.

The question irked Soojin enough to make her sit up. "I don't hate the idea of going. I just don't want to move there. I want to stay here, with Appa and all my friends. Why can't you understand that?"

Eomma reached over to take Soojin's hand in both of hers and press it tightly. "You really do love it here, don't you?"

"This is my home," Soojin replied simply.

Eomma closed her eyes for a long moment. Then she let out a deep breath. "I think I made a big mistake," she said. "I rushed to make a decision that I thought was right without understanding how it would affect you."

Soojin stared at her mother in surprise.

"I have been so narrow-minded and focused on only the bad things that have happened to us, without remembering all the good. Today, I was reminded that there are many different kinds of Americans."

Soojin nodded cautiously. "Appa always said there are more good Americans than bad ones."

"And you can handle all of them." Eomma smiled. "Because you're an American also. You belong here." She scooted her chair to Soojin's side and reached over to hug her. "Soojin, I'm so sorry."

Soojin felt a flutter of hope. "Does that mean we're not moving to Korea?" she asked.

"I never had a real plan," Eomma admitted ruefully. "All I knew was that I needed to see my family and wanted to get away, so I could think."

"So . . . we weren't actually moving? We were going to come back?" Soojin was confused.

Eomma turned her hand palm-side up. "I don't know. I was angry and upset. I miss Korea. But watching you be so strong today makes me realize I've been trying to run away from my problems. That's not fair to you or your father."

Eomma smiled at Soojin. "Your home is here, and my home is with you and your dad."

The pain in her chest subsided; still, Soojin frowned. "But you said you hate it here."

"Ah, I was angry, Soojin," her mother replied. "I get scared sometimes, but I don't really hate it here. There are many good things about America—things I love. While I have a lot to think about, I will get over my anger. But I think I deserve time in Korea with my parents, don't you?"

Soojin nodded enthusiastically.

"Good. Then we'll spend the summer in Seoul with our relatives and come back in time for the start of school. How does that sound?"

"Thank you, Eomma!" Soojin hugged her mother tightly, smiling so hard, she felt like her face would split open.

She wasn't moving to Korea.

She was going to visit, and then she'd come home to America.

"Hi! Remember me? I'm the manager at the Garrett stand." Soojin blinked in surprise to see someone standing next to them. It was the pretty cashier who had sold

Soojin her popcorn. "We heard about what happened, and we wanted to make sure you got some more Garrett Mix before your flight."

Soojin's mouth hung open in surprise. "How'd you hear about it?"

"Oh, my friend Angie told me." She handed Soojin a large blue-and-silver-striped tin bucket. "Here is a gift for you to share," she said. Then she held out a smaller plastic bag full of popcorn. "And this little bag is for you to eat all by yourself."

Soojin gasped. "This is all for me?"

"We want you to know that Chicago is a great city, and we'd love to have you back," the manager said.

Soojin nodded enthusiastically. "Oh yes! It sure is! Thank you so much!"

She hugged the tin and waved goodbye to the Garrett manager. Once again, she could smell the sweet-and-salty buttery aroma of the popcorn. She felt almost light-headed with relief.

Eomma looked so surprised that Soojin had to laugh. She was full of sheer joy, feeling so different from when she'd stood in front of that map earlier, staring at the circle that said *You are here* and wishing she wasn't. At this moment in time, she was so happy to be here, in this airport, with her mother and this big tin of Garrett popcorn. Tomorrow, that circle would be in Korea, but it wouldn't be there forever.

She couldn't wait to call Appa and tell him that this trip wasn't permanent. That she'd be coming home in a few weeks.

Back to New York, where she belonged.

A Note from the Editor

Dear Reader,

I'm so glad you've chosen to read *You Are Here*. There are a lot of other people who are also happy you did so—especially the other eleven authors who have written some pretty marvelous stories for this book. And you should know that working with these writers has been an amazing process filled with warmth and laughter and lots of bonding. Because this is a project we all really believe in. And these pages are filled with so much truth, as well as a lot of hope for a better tomorrow.

Now that you've read *You Are Here*, you might have some questions. Hopefully, I can help you understand more about the project through a little bit of history and backstory and an explanation about why we felt the need to come together to make this book.

What is an Asian American?
Clearly, it is a very vague term. How can it be otherwise when Asia is not only the largest continent in the world, but it also has the biggest population? And the forty-seven to fifty countries (seriously, the number changes depending on what source you check!) that make up this vast land

are divided into East, South, West, Central, and Southeast Asia. There's a lot of fascinating history behind the term "Asian American": Did you know that it has only been in existence since 1968, and it was created by the activists Emma Gee and Yuji Ichioka, who needed a name for their political action group? The idea was to unite all the subgroups of "Asians" to fight together for greater equality! So, while the term "Asian American" is broad, its roots are in an organized response to political and socioeconomic issues, and it's important to remember that in the wider fight against racism and prejudice.

Why does this book focus on East and Southeast Asian Americans?

The idea for this book started with an anthology I edited, called *Flying Lessons and Other Stories*, for We Need Diverse Books (WNDB), a nonprofit I cofounded back in 2014 that is dedicated to advocating for more diversity in children's literature. *Flying Lessons* featured a wonderful array of diverse representation and received wide acclaim, including five starred reviews, and we were all so proud of it. But then a blogger reached out to me to express how disappointed they were by the East Asian representation in the book. I was surprised. We had included a fantastic story about a girl pirate by Grace Lin. But the blogger pointed out that the story was set in China, while all the other stories in *Flying Lessons* were about American kids. Our only East Asian story was one that othered Asian Americans. It was a shocking revelation for both Grace and me to realize what we had unconsciously done. And it became a priority for us to address it and to create a book that recognized the uniqueness of the East Asian American experience.

Since then, a lot has happened, notably the COVID-19 pandemic and the very specific anti-Asian sentiment that came along with it. There was a huge increase in reports of violent hate crimes against Asian Americans that were directly related to misinformation about the disease. While racism against all Asians increased, language like "China Virus," "Kung Flu," and "Go back to China" directly targeted anyone who looked East or Southeast Asian. The need for this book became all the more urgent, and its scope grew to address the larger issues. Books can be important discussion starters, and I've always believed that diverse children's books with authentic representation are both our weapons and our defense against prejudice, because children's books teach empathy.

Why does the book take place in an airport?
Great question! It was Minh Lê's idea to use an airport for the setting because it was a logical place for a whole lot of

different people from all over the country to cross paths. And there is something vibrant and exciting about an airport: it's a place full of comings and goings and countless intersections.

Why Chicago?
We wanted a city with a big, busy international airport, so people could be flying in from everywhere. But most important, Chicago is home to Garrett popcorn, which is my favorite!

How did you decide which authors you'd ask to contribute?
So, the very first person I approached was Grace Lin, because we had been talking about this idea since *Flying Lessons*, and I knew how much the project meant to her. Then I asked Linda Sue Park, because she is not only like an eonni (big sister) to me, she is an icon of children's literature who is also a fantastic person. After that . . . well, the truth is, I asked writers for whom I have insane amounts of respect and admiration and who are also great people. Because I knew we would all have to work really closely together. Over the months of creating this book, we exchanged countless emails and calls and met together virtually to plan the book and hash out details, and I can truly say that our Zoom meetings were an absolute pleasure. My only regret is that I

couldn't ask more authors to join us for this project! There are a ton of other awesome writers and so many more stories to be told about Asian Americans, both within the East and Southeast Asian American communities and beyond them. I hope this book will inspire even more stories!

Thank you for joining us on this journey through twelve different looks at the Asian American experience. For some of you, the events represented here will come as an eye-opening surprise, while others of you will recognize elements of your own lives in these pages. But at the core of this book is a reminder that Asian Americans are Americans, too. We belong here. We are part of the fabric and history of this country that we love dearly, and this book is both an affirmation and a celebration of who we are.

Meet the Authors

Traci Chee is Chinese and Japanese American, and her family, like her character Natalie's, has been in the United States for more than a hundred years. A *New York Times* bestselling author and National Book Award finalist, she is the author of such books as *A Thousand Steps into Night*, *We Are Not Free*, and The Reader trilogy. When she isn't at her computer or snuggled up with a book, she enjoys hiking, egg painting, gardening, and hosting game nights for family and friends. She lives in California with her fast dog.

Mike Chen, who is Chinese American, started piano lessons when he was five years old, before picking up guitar at thirteen. Despite all those years of playing music, he's probably not as skilled at guitar as his character Lee is. In his twenties, Mike played in bands and DJ'd before trying something just as cool: becoming a writer. He is the author of books including *Here and Now and Then*, *We Could Be Heroes*, *Light Years from Home*, and *Star Wars: Brotherhood*, and he contributes to geek media sites such as StarTrek.com, Nerdist, and Tor.com. Mike lives in the Bay Area with his wife and daughter. He is very proud of his daughter's love of Siouxsie and the Banshees.

Both **Meredith Ireland** and her character Mindy are Korean American adoptees who grew up in New York City. Meredith's parents were a nurse and a librarian—and they weren't *really* "inquisitive." She loves oatmeal with brown sugar and thinks P.F. Chang's is pretty good. Meredith is also really bad with learning foreign languages, despite her degrees from Rollins College and the University of Miami School of Law. She's the author of *The Jasmine Project* and *Everyone Hates Kelsie Miller*, both of which proudly feature adopted main characters. She is also the mother of two children and a carnival goldfish who will outlive them all.

Mike Jung is both Korean American and autistic like his character Henry, but he is also significantly taller, possibly due to being 333 percent older. He also shares Henry's affinity for aikido, cats, donuts, and (obviously) books, and generously incorporates them all into his mysterious and intriguing existence in Oakland, California, where he lives with the woman whose husband he is, the two kids whom he played the easy part in bringing into the world, and their cat, who does as he pleases. Mike can legitimately claim to be the award-winning author of books including *Unidentified Suburban Object* and *The Boys in the Back Row* and a contributor to acclaimed anthologies such as *The Hero Next Door*, but he is far too self-effacing to actually say so.

Also, he's lying about that last part: dude is super, super braggy.

Erin Entrada Kelly grew up in Louisiana, less than an hour from the Texas border. Much as her character Camilla does, she once had to haul a fifty-pound suitcase to the Philippines on a journey that lasted nearly forty hours. When she was Greta's age, she wanted to hide, though she never wore baseball caps. Erin doesn't like to hide anymore. She is now a *New York Times* bestselling author. She has received the 2018 Newbery Medal for *Hello, Universe*, a 2021 Newbery Honor for *We Dream of Space*, the 2017 Asian/Pacific American Award for Literature, and many other honors. She lives in Delaware.

Minh Lê spent much of his childhood (and to be honest, his adulthood, too) grappling with his relationship to Vietnamese culture and language—in fact, he even wrote a book about it called *Drawn Together*, which won the 2019 Asian/Pacific American Award for Literature. So he totally gets why Khoi is so anxious while waiting for his flight. Minh's other books include the Eisner-nominated *Lift* and the middle grade graphic novel *Green Lantern: Legacy*. He has several forthcoming projects, including *A Lotus for You*, the authorized biography of the late Zen Buddhist monk and Nobel Peace Prize nominee Thích Nhất Hạnh. In addition to books, Minh has written about children's literature for a variety of publications, including National Public Radio (NPR), the *Huffington Post*, and the *New York Times*.

Grace Lin is a Taiwanese American who, like her character Jane, spent a lot of her childhood with SAT practice test books. Unlike Jane, however, Grace would fill in the SAT practice questions by surreptitiously sneaking the answers from the back of the book. She then spent the time she was supposed to be "studying for the SATs" reading fairy tales and drawing unicorns, which has worked out pretty well for her. Grace is now an award-winning and *New York Times* bestselling author-illustrator of many books, from picture books to novels, including her Newbery Honor Book, *Where the Mountain Meets the Moon*, and her Caldecott Honor Book, *A Big Mooncake for Little Star*. She is an occasional commentator for TEDx Talks and the PBS NewsHour, and hosts two podcasts: *Book Friends Forever* and *Kids Ask Authors*. In 2016, Grace was recognized by President Barack Obama's office as a Champion of Change for Asian American and Pacific Islander Art and Storytelling, and in 2022, the ALA honored Grace with the Children's Literature Legacy Award.

Ellen Oh is Korean American and has a lot in common with her character Soojin. She, too, worked in her family's deli/grocery store in Brooklyn, New York. She loves K-pop and K-dramas, and can eat an entire tin of Garrett popcorn by herself. Ellen actually did attend New York University and then Georgetown University Law Center, where she met her husband, who refused to move to New York City, causing Ellen to permanently move to the Maryland suburbs right outside Washington, DC. She's a recovering attorney and an award-winning author of books including *Finding Junie Kim*, *The Dragon Egg Princess*, and the Spirit Hunters series, as well as the editor of *Flying Lessons and Other Stories*. The only thing she loves more than Garrett popcorn is Krispy Kreme donuts.

Linda Sue Park is the daughter of Korean immigrants. Like her character Jae, she makes too many impulsive decisions, is often confused about what it means to be good, and thinks that being bored is the worst. She has written more than two dozen books for young readers, including the 2002 Newbery Medal winner, *A Single Shard*, and the *New York Times* bestseller *A Long Walk to Water*. Linda Sue is the founder and curator of Allida Books, an imprint of HarperCollins. She serves on the advisory boards of We Need Diverse Books and the Rabbit hOle children's literature museum project and created the kiBooka website to celebrate authors and illustrators of Korean descent. She loves cooking, eating, snorkeling, watching baseball, playing games on her phone, and vacationing with family and friends (preferably in places where she can snorkel). Linda Sue knows very well that she will never be able to read every great book ever written, but she keeps trying anyway.

Randy Ribay is a biracial Filipino American and, like his character AJ, played in a Fil-Am basketball league when he was in middle school. Also like AJ, Randy was solidly second string. He eventually went on to study English literature at the University of Colorado at Boulder and then became a teacher. After earning his master's degree in language and literacy at the Harvard Graduate School of Education, Randy continued teaching and began writing stories. He's the author of *An Infinite Number of Parallel Universes*, *After the Shot Drops*, and *Patron Saints of Nothing*, which was a National Book Award finalist. He currently lives in the San Francisco Bay Area with his wife, son, and adorable dogs.

Christina Soontornvat is a Thai American author of award-winning books for children, including *A Wish in the Dark* and *All Thirteen: The Incredible Cave Rescue of the Thai Boys' Soccer Team*, which were both named Newbery

Honor Books. Like her character Paul, Christina has made many overseas trips to visit her family in Thailand, and (also like Paul) she hates all the waiting involved. Paul's tale is inspired by a true story of returning a loved one's remains to the place where their heart belongs. Christina grew up behind the counter of her parents' Thai restaurant with her nose stuck in a book. She currently lives in Austin, Texas, with her husband, two rascally cats, and two even rascally-ier daughters.

Susan Tan is from a mixed-race Chinese American and Jewish family, just like her characters Ari and Ezzie. She also once got her finger stuck in an airport chair (oops!). Along with being a writer, Susan is an assistant professor at University of Massachusetts Boston, where she spends her days talking about books and waving her hands wildly while she does (because books are so exciting!). She lives in Cambridge, Massachusetts, and loves to knit and crochet. Susan's books include the Cilla Lee-Jenkins series, the Pets Rule! series, and *Ghosts, Toast, and Other Hazards*.

Marcos Chin amazed all the authors by brilliantly bringing their characters to life on the beautiful cover of *You Are Here*. A Chinese Canadian artist, Marcos was born in Mozambique, Africa, moved to Portugal, and grew up in

Canada. He now lives in Brooklyn, New York, where he draws for himself and for such clients as Starbucks, Honda, Banana Republic, Google, and the *New York Times*. Marcos's illustrations are inspired by the people around him. In addition to drawing, Marcos loves fashion, the outdoors, and traveling to warm places that are close to a beach.

All the authors wish to thank Allida and the HarperCollins team for all the amazing support, love, and care that has gone into every step of this book. We couldn't have done it without our wonderful team!! Thank you to Linda Sue Park, Anne Hoppe, Mary Wilcox, Jamie Ryu, Jessie Gang, Alison Klapthor, Alison Donalty, Erika West, Mary Magrisso, Christine Ma, Susan Bishansky, Trish McGinley, Abigail Marks, Caitlin Garing, Lauren Levite, John Sellers, Vaishali Nayak, Delaney Heisterkamp, Robert Imfeld, Lisa DiSarro, Julie Yeater, Patty Rosati and Mimi Rankin and their whole team, and the awesome HarperCollins Children's Book sales force. We would also like to thank Marietta Zacker, who believed in us from the start.